'Tis the season to be daring...

the 12 dares of Christmas

Leigh W. Stuart

CITY OWL
PRESS

THE 12 DARES OF CHRISTMAS

CITY OWL PRESS
www.cityowlpress.com

Cover Design by Tina Moss and Mary Cain. All stock photos licensed appropriately.

Edited by Mary Cain.

For information on subsidiary rights, please contact the publisher at info@cityowlpress.com.

Print Edition ISBN: 978-1-944728-10-6

Digital Edition ISBN: 978-1-5365-9719-6

Printed in the United States of America

For my husband —

friend, fellow adventurer and love of my life.

You are always there to make me laugh, fix the electronics,

and be my hero down the toughest roads.

- Leigh

Chapter 1

He was late.

Lauren's star performer of the evening was late, and by the looks of the snow piling up outside the hotel, he was either cozied up in some love nest because he had forgotten his promise or he was freezing to death in his car in an icy ditch. Either way, she couldn't reach him by phone and he hadn't tried to contact her. Relying on a friend of a friend's cousin might have been free, but it hadn't been smart.

When the snow started falling at noon, she should have known something would go wrong tonight. The fortune cookie that came with her lunch had warned her: *You learn from your mistakes. You will learn a lot today.* She'd written it off as crummy prophesizing at its finest. She wouldn't be making any mistakes.

Lauren pulled the slip of paper out of her pants and tore it into shreds, then she wadded the shreds in a ball and threw it on the floor.

One mistake so far. She swallowed a scream and settled

for stomping her foot. No more. She had reached her quota.

What were the odds she could find another a male dancer to jump out of a cake in the next fifteen minutes?

Lauren paced, checking her phone every time she turned and ignoring the nausea spreading through her stomach. The small changing room off the hotel lobby only gave her enough space to take a few steps before she had to turn, and there was less and less air. In the ballroom down the hall, over two dozen ladies waited for the evening's entertainment she had promised to provide.

They were depending on her, and she owed them for all the help they had given. These ladies had busted their bums to raise money for her project the last couple of months.

She reached for the door at the same time it flew open.

Abby popped in, alone. "The dinner is fab, but they'll be into the desserts soon. Any news?"

Lauren shook her head. Her phone screen remained abysmally dark and lifeless. "Nothing yet."

"Call him again. Do something. These ladies are starting to prowl like caged lions in there, and it's not going to be pretty if they don't get something to appease their appetites soon, if you know what I mean."

Lauren's stomach twisted into a knot. "Keep stalling. All right?"

Abby shook her hair, revealing green and red stripes under the blond. She shut the door, leaving Lauren sinking in her unworthiness.

The Knitting Society of Sycamore Cove deserved this gesture.

Several months ago when Lauren first contacted groups and businesses in town to ask for support for the shelter, the knitters jumped at the opportunity to give back to their community. They wanted to branch out and change their image as stuffy old ladies who sat around, buried in yarn and drinking tea into dynamic do-gooders. After giving the cause their everything, Lauren thought they should have an especially fun end-of-the-year party. The society's president agreed. A male dancer would be the whipped cream and a cherry to the evening.

Maybe there was a reason she couldn't find a job in her field of studies and had been stuck as a waitress since graduating with her bachelor's degree. Or maybe she simply needed to try harder. Lauren needed to show Sycamore Cove, and herself, that she was positively ingenious.

She did what any young woman in need of a hot, male stripper would do.

No, scratch that. She did exactly the opposite of what a young woman in this situation would do. Finding her brother's number in her contacts, she made her second mistake of the evening.

"Hey, Cooper, it's me. I'm in a bit of bind and could use your help tonight."

Cheers and yells blared in the background. "I'm kind of busy right now."

"Yeah. I understand. Remember that time you busted Mom's crystal vase in the entryway and you blamed it on neighbor kids, and got me to back up your story? Get over here and help me with the cake or I'm telling her."

"Is this...blackmail?"

"Be in the Portside Hotel lobby in ten minutes, or I'm calling Mom to ruin her cruise." Lauren's conscious twinged at blackmailing her brother. Then she remembered the time he shaved her Barbie's' heads.

No mercy in the Hall family.

Abby crashed through the door, snapping her back to the here and now. "They are antsy for the surprise, Lauren. What do we do?"

"Stall them. I have a guy coming, I promise."

"That sounds so promising the way you say 'guy.' How about, the 'hunky male dancer' is coming? That has a much nicer ring to it," Abby said. "Don't forget, I have popcorn for us and these little sparkly-confetti shooters."

"Keep your bra fastened. Our cake *guy* will be here in less than ten minutes. I'm taking a rain check on this performance, though." Watch her brother jump out of a cake and start to shimmy? Yuck.

"Suit yourself." Abby waved her confetti shooter on her way out. "I'm off to stall. Some more."

This would work.

Lauren had a *Singing in the Rain*-style cake, a pair of free stripper pants (one size fits most) and edible body oil—eggnog flavored for the holidays—ready to go. All she needed was a 'stud-muffin,' as the knitting society president had put it.

Her brother would have to do. Most women found him studdly, at least.

Lauren collapsed in a fold-out chair, holding her head. The sounds of Christmas cheer filtered in from the ballroom. She had to pull this off. This town needed a new animal shelter—one with a no-kill policy and clean, roomy kennels—and she intended to prove she was capable of organizing projects for the betterment of society. Each minute that passed crawled on prickly pin-needle legs down her back.

Come on, Cooper, where—?

"I'm looking for Lauren Hall," a husky, male voice said at the check-in counter. "There should be a cake…"

"That's me," she cried, running out. The friend of a friend's cousin had arrived. "That's me, I'm—" She halted her headlong flight, nearly slipping on the polished tiles.

Holy smoke from a Yuletide fire, her Christmas wishes

had been granted. And then some.

A mouthwatering ginger with a trim beard and captivating, green eyes stepped toward her. Broad shoulders filled his wool coat, jeans hugged his narrow waist, and melting snow twinkled in his hair, lashes, and beard. He could be the sexy poster boy for the town's tourist industry.

Those ladies wouldn't know what hit them. They'd be knitting ties and crocheting handcuffs for him to tie them up with in no time. However, Lauren had a job to do. She stood as tall as her five-foot-one-inch'" frame and three-inch heels would allow, and told the hyperactive butterflies in her stomach to take the party elsewhere. Time to crack the whip, but sadly not the kinky kind.

He held out a hand. "Nice to finally meet you, I'm—"

"Here to make me a very happy woman," Lauren said. Craning her neck, she smiled up at him. "Let's get you out of those clothes."

***

Gabe turned at the words 'That's me!' to introduce himself. And his brain stumbled to a halt. Lauren Hall. His nerves buzzed as she hurtled toward him, a sizzling fireball of energy and excitement. Silky brown curls, pillowed lips in a wide smile, form-hugging black pants and white blouse begging to be unbuttoned. A rush surged through him, like diving in a pool for a race. The same shock of cold that electrified every inch of him and set him on fire for the chase.

Shit. He should have put on a better sweater. More cologne. An extra layer of deodorant.

Instincts jolted him to action.

"Nice to finally meet you, I'm—"

"Here to make me a very happy woman," Lauren interrupted, not waiting for his name. Cooper must have told her he was coming. Her smile knocked him senseless again. "Let's get you out of those clothes."

It was all he could do to play it cool. The second she grabbed his hand, muscles through his back and stomach tightened and his heart kicked his ribs, sending blood to his woefully neglected lower extremities. Yeah. Those extremities perked right up.

He'd seen pictures of her, of course. Except the ones Cooper had shown him were of a younger, awkward high school girl and college student. The Lauren currently dragging him down a hallway was an entirely different story. She was all woman. Following behind, he admired the curves of her short stature. Her rich brown hair fell in loose curls to her shoulders, ready for him to lace his fingers through.

Cooper hadn't talked much about his little sister over the years, except to mention having to beat up any guys sniffing around her or brag how much of herself she gave to her social causes. In his eyes, she was right up there with St. Teresa, but more untouchable.

Preconceived notions about the laid-back, friendly evening he had anticipated were thrown out the window by the eager pull on his hand. She seemed to have something in mind for him, and who was he to argue when a pretty girl told him to take his clothes off?

He had readily accepted when Cooper asked if he could lend a hand. He was still riding high from how well his interview had gone earlier that afternoon. His luck was changing from being laid off with no warning to stumbling on the perfect opportunity to move up as an analytics manager with the governor's staff in Richmond. And now a very attractive woman was escorting him to a glorified closet with the promise of nudity.

The holidays just got a whole lot more enchanting.

"In here." She motioned for him to enter the small room. Her cheeks were flushed deeper than before.

He stepped through the doorway, closer to her than absolutely necessary, and breathed in her floral-and-spices scent. Sugar. There was something very sweet in the room. Or the scent could be coming from her. His mouth watered.

"Where do we start?" He inspected the room. No cakes. In fact, not much of anything at all besides a box wrapped in plastic.

She closed the door, sliding sideways. Determined hands tugged at his coat. "We have to get you ready and in a hurry."

"Hurry?" His coat flew toward the table.

She darted out from behind him. "I am so happy you showed up when you did, but I needed you ready ten minutes ago."

"Let's get rolling, then." He rubbed his hands together, not that they needed warming. He couldn't stop the grin determined to take over his face.

"That's what I like to hear. I believe in jumping in and getting things done." She pointed toward the corner. "There's a changing curtain so you can get out of your street clothes. And I have edible body oil. It's eggnog-flavored."

"Edible, eggnog-flavored body oil?" And now his winter evening just got warmer.

"Yes. If you want it. To help with your performance, of course."

Performance? He swallowed a cough, clearing his throat. She didn't need to worry about his *performance*. Heat spiraled up from his center. He stepped closer, and the white tube she was waving landed lightly on his chest.

She blinked up at him. Her sweet smell wafted over him. He couldn't wait to get a taste. "Did you want it?"

"That depends on who's putting it on me," he said.

Her lips rounded in an 'O'. "You want me to… All right. Let's do it."

"I'd be more than happy to put it on you as well." He covered her hand with his own, loving how it fit under his larger one and the way she arched her back to look at him.

"Really? But later. Much later. Your clothes have to come off first," she said.

"You really want me out of these clothes, don't you?"

"Yes! Well, no. Not for me personally, but for the animals. That is, I don't want to take advantage of you by getting a freebie, although I am grateful you are doing this for free."

"Doing what for free?" Lending a hand for some cake situation, as Cooper had called it? As if he would charge her money for that.

"A striptease, of course."

He froze. She hadn't been joking about getting him out of his clothes. Not in the least. All the blood rushing to his extremities reached its final destination and he strained painfully against his jeans. An alarm went off somewhere in his head, but it was distant and easy to ignore.

He let go of her hand and tugged his sweater up and off. It fell to the floor. He stepped forward, closing the distance between them.

"First the clothes and then the oil, is that correct?" His voice came out ragged, her unexpected request trumping his self-control.

Tipping her head to meet his gaze, she fanned herself with her hand. "Sounds about right to me. Although, you can go behind the curtain if you're bashful, which would be odd in your line of…Santa's reindeers…" Her voice trailed off, but he hadn't been listening.

The next article of clothing to go had been his t-shirt, which landed with a swoosh next to the sweater.

"Is getting close and personal part of your act? It is really effective." Her gaze was riveted to his chest and torso. The extra swim time he had put in lately was paying off.

"This isn't an act."

"You probably say that all the time." She was breathing as fast as a last-minute shopper running through stores on Christmas Eve. "Listen, to be sure, can you keep it up for half an hour?"

"Beg pardon?"

"A half an hour. Can you go for that long?" She opened the tube of body oil.

Images of all the things he could do to her while armed with the flavored oil sent him reeling. Only half an hour? "I can keep it up for longer than that, I promise."

"It's not too hard?"

He moved in close enough to feel her body heat, the scent of her perfume and sugary sweetness growing stronger. She gasped, stepping back until she hit the door, but her chest rose in invitation as he invaded her space. He placed his arms on either side of her to pin her in. Her lips were sinfully moist and eyes heavily lidded.

"It's hard," he breathed in her ear.

"Really? Any way I can make it easier on you?"

So many ways raced through his brain. He inhaled to enumerate a few of his favorites, but then another thought hit.

This was his best friend's sister. He couldn't strip and engage in mutual oil rubbing. It went against all the rules in the guy handbook, despite the fact she was sober and clearly knew what she wanted.

Cooper's invitation for him to stay for a week, after his job interview in Richmond, might have included the promise of drinking, partying, and playing the field, but the *field* didn't exactly include Cooper's sister.

She shivered, tilting her head to give him a better view of her neck and velvet earlobe. That he wanted to nibble on.

To hell with the guy handbook. Best friend's little sister or not, when a beautiful brunette brought out the body oil, all bets were off.

"Tell me—"

Lauren was shoved roughly from behind. He reached instinctively as she fell forward, wrapping her in his arms to keep her from crashing to the floor. Something wet splattered his chest. Cinnamon, nutmeg, and creamy vanilla filled the air.

The door had been forced open, and a wild-eyed blonde poked her head through.

"Whoa, who blocked the door? Where's the cake, for the love of consumerism? And what are you doing—" The irritation in her expression melted into surprise. "I'm interrupting something, aren't I?"

The blonde's eyes fell on him and stayed locked there. "The cake man. Wow, I am so glad to see you. Ah, Lauren, get it together and get this show on the road, right?"

"Abby," Lauren yelled. She pushed free of Gabe's hold. He let go, reluctantly saying good-bye to her soft breasts that had been pressed against him. "Two minutes. Two minutes!"

She began to shut the door, but Abby reached through and grabbed her. "Do you know how much he charges for private shows?"

"Out!"

Slam!

"Private shows?" Gabe asked.

"Ignore her, please." Her gaze, which had been locked on his chest, flitted to the bottle of oil in her hand and back. "Oil problem solved."

He stepped back. See-through blotches covered her breasts and white bra.

Lauren continued to stare, mouth open. Streaks of gleaming oil ran in rivulets across his chest and into his jeans.

Her gaze devoured the length of his chest and then climbed inch by inch up, the heat in it going from spring in Greenland to full-blown heat wave in Georgia. She caught him watching her and a flush stained her cheeks.

"Did you come prepared for tonight, or do I need to loan you a...something to *wear*?"

Strange emphasis on *wear*. Had he come prepared? It was a good question in case things got really hot. "Yes, I have one in my wallet."

"'One'?"

"We can get more later. I agree, one won't be enough," he said.

"Wait, what are we talking about? What exactly do you have in your wallet?"

"A condom."

"One condom? What are you going to do with a condom? There are two dozen women in the other room waiting for you," she said.

He took a slow step backward.

"Two"—he choked—"dozen women?"

"Yes, the Sycamore Cove Knitting Society. Didn't your cousin explain the show?"

"My cousin arranged a show?" *I'll kill him.*

"Why do you think you're here? But thank goodness you showed up. Would you believe I actually called my brother to blackmail him into doing the show?"

"Your brother?" he asked. "And the cake is...?"

"There." She pointed to a large object in the corner, covered with a plastic sheet. "So if your jeans aren't part of the show, let's get them off you."

Those words were seriously less thrilling than they should

have been. He and Lauren were *not* on the same page. "What exactly was your brother going to do with the cake?"

"Pop out of it, of course. You don't know my brother, but it would have been the highlight of the decade for me to make him do it. No offense to you and your line of work, but paybacks are hell, and he owes me big-time. No problem, I have a spare set of tear-away pants you can wear."

All he could do was blink, processing the term "tear-away pants." The situation was souring. "Lauren, there's something I'd like to clear up."

"Oh shit. You know my brother and you're afraid of him, aren't you?"

"I'm not afraid of Cooper, no."

"Great. Okay. We are running so late. Jeans off, *now*." She grabbed a bundle of shiny fake leather and shoved it in his hands.

The doorknob jiggled, and the blonde stuck her head in again, hissing Lauren's name.

"That wasn't two minutes. Give us the full two minutes," Lauren snapped.

"Our ladies are getting antsy. They finished dinner and they want their hunk delivered."

"Okay, we really have to talk," Gabe said.

"No, we really have to get ready. See you out there," Lauren said, pushing the other woman out. "And have one of the bellhops come get the cake!" She shut the door, turning her flushed face to his. "Do you think those will fit? They're a one-size-fits-most."

With the blood returning to his body and more importantly, his brain, things were finally adding up. Street clothes, body oil, two dozen women, and a really big cake.

If the ladies were finished with dinner, he was supposed to be their dessert.

He flipped open the bundle and snapped the fabric to reveal a pair of slim pants with press buttons down the sides. A red thong was included. A stringy, red man-thong with a big pouch hanging from the middle. He held it up between his fingertips for inspection.

"Lauren Hall," he said, regret bitter on his tongue, "I'd like to introduce myself. I'm Gabe Nicholson, your brother Cooper's friend from college. He sent me to help you with a cake, but I doubt this is what he meant."

"Gabe." Her mouth dropped open after saying his name. Blood drained from her cheeks. "Cooper's friend, Gabe? You don't look at all like the pictures I've seen. That also means you're not...not...the friend of my friend's cousin? Valentino il Grande?"

"No, I'm not."

"Oh, sweet potato pie. Then you're not the semiprofessional male dancer who loves animals and came tonight as a big favor?" She clenched her hands, a grimace marring her features.

"No. I'm sorry."

"How would you like to become the amateur male dancer who loves animals and is doing me a big favor?"

"I don't think so, no." Gabe's love for animals only went so far.

"Not even to save kittens?"

"Look, I don't want to upset you, but this..." He shook his head. Putting on those pants and climbing in a cake wasn't happening. He drew the line at threatening the future of his career.

"I'll pay you."

He moved to go.

"Wait, I have—" She rushed to her bag to find her wallet. Bills and coins spilled on the table as she counted. "Twenty-three fifty in cash, and maybe more tomorrow!"

"I would gladly take you out for a drink later, or save kittens in danger with you, but this?"

Grabbing his arms to prevent him from putting on his shirt, she gazed up at him. Soulful, coffee-bean-brown eyes blinked up at him, weakening his resolve. *She must practice that look in a mirror.* "I'm begging you, Gabe. You aren't chicken, are you? You think these little old ladies will attack you?"

"No," he said, spine stiffening. He was afraid of some things, but showing women a good time wasn't one of them. "I'm no chicken."

"Prove it. Go out there and show those grannies what you showed me here." She took a deep breath. "I dare you."

Chapter 2

From the dangerous spark in Gabe's eyes, Lauren knew she'd made another mistake. Her pulse throbbed in her head and she wiped her sweaty hands on her slacks. Gabe was her brother's college roommate and they'd been on the swim team together. She had seen pictures of him on Facebook. Holy holly, he was one of Cooper's best friends. How had she not recognized him? And she'd thought he was a stripper! Wait. How many mistakes did that make? She refused to count them anymore.

Dammit, if he didn't go for the dare, she wouldn't have anyone to put in the cake.

"You...dare me?" One corner of his mouth quirked up. Those smooth lips were incredibly sexy in a half smile.

No going back now. "I dare you. I dare you to put on these pants, get in that cake, and jump up, rocking the world of the women in the next room. After that, I need you to try to make the fun last for at least twenty minutes. I promise they'll treat you right. They'll most likely be glued to their seats the whole time or passing out in the first five minutes." She bit her lower lip.

"You dare me." He unbuttoned his jeans, knocking her breathless. "You know I get to dare you next, right?"

"Really? I mean, right. Nothing illegal, nothing harmful, and nothing—" She was going to say "'humiliating,'" but her dare was in a gray zone. "And nothing morally reprehensible."

He held up the red thong. "Because the pouch on these just screams 'upstanding morals'?"

"If you're going to do it, please hurry. You can change behind the curtain."

"And now you tell me about the curtain."

"Technically I mentioned the curtain earlier." She bounced in place, trying to loosen the knot in her stomach. At this point she would agree to anything.

Gabe disappeared behind the curtain. A few scuffling noises and a groan followed.

"Does it fit?" Lauren called.

"I'm not sure the issue here is whether or not it fits, but how easy it is to pull off," Gabe said from behind the curtain.

"Then let me see it." The way her day was going, the cake people had given her a pair of faulty stripper pants.

More rustling followed and the curtain billowed as Gabe moved around. His black-clad calves and bare feet shifted as he turned in a slow circle.

"You asked for it." He drew back the curtain.

Lauren's legs loosened from ankle to thigh.

Bare-chested and in faux-leather pants that didn't leave an inch of him to the imagination, he was stunning. Did she mention how little the pants left to the imagination? Not a single glorious inch. Her nipples tightened at the thought of those inches.

He gave her a crooked grin and ran his hands through his ginger locks, biceps and triceps flexing. His chest and stomach rippled like rings on a pond, drawing the eye downward to his sculpted thighs and well, what could only be described as a well-endowed bulge in his pants.

"Is there a problem?" Lauren asked. There weren't any problems as far as she could tell. She would have continued, but her jaw wasn't working and she realized she was addressing his chest. She moved her eyes up until she made contact with his. Her jaw still wouldn't work.

Tugging his waistband, he clicked his tongue when several buttons at his hips popped open. "See?"

Lauren shook her head.

"I can't sit down or move without these pants falling off."

"And that's a problem because, why?" She was on the verge of tugging them off herself. Just as a test, of course.

"When I jump out of the cake, I'll already be pantsless."

"It's a moot point. Your audience won't be picky. Tonight is a fun get-together for some lovely women who raised a ton of money for a new animal shelter, and they simply deserve a good time."

"So I'm just a good time for a bunch of women?" He folded his arms and leaned back.

A dry spot on his shoulder was in need of some oil. Her hands itched to fix it. *Focus, Lauren, focus! Get him in the cake.*

"If you're too chicken, now is the time so say it. Otherwise—" Someone knocked at the door, and she hiccupped in surprise. "This is it. Let's get this show rolling!"

***

Gabe could kiss any job at the governor's office—or any government job for that matter—good-bye if a video leaked of what was about to happen.

For more than two years he'd sat at a desk shoved up against the rattling elevator, reporting strings of statistics to a backstabbing boss, and working his ass off for a promotion that never came.

He needed this job. Numbers from his bank account ran through his head.

What could he use as a good stripper name, just in case pictures of this went viral? What had she called the guy who didn't show up? Valentino il Grande. He would need a name like that in the event he had to take his life in a new direction…

Dietrich VonSchlong?

Sebastian Easy Rider?

Jackhammer Jones?

Andre the Giant? No, that one was already taken.

Or more Latin lover? Romeo, Eduardo, or Vittorio?

No, something more mountain man: Dean Everest, Hart Woodsman, Seth Bearskin.

No.

Shit on a brick. *What the hell am I doing?*

The cake was much smaller than he expected. Were male strippers usually short and skinny? That didn't seem right.

He was insane, but when she had dared him, he couldn't resist the possibilities that opened up in front of him.

He shifted, trying to get comfortable. What the hell was he going to do when he popped out of this thing? Sure, he could entertain one or even two women at a time, but two dozen?

***

Lauren wondered how he would keep his pants buttoned until he popped up, and then how long before one of the lovely elderly knitters yanked them off.

He'd made her promise not to take pictures, not to tell anyone his name, or to post anything on YouTube. Some issue about keeping his image clean because getting some new job depended on it.

He didn't say anything about not taking pictures for her own use. She patted her hip, checking for her phone. It was there and waiting for her.

Lauren handed the cake off to the bellhop and hurried into the ballroom. Abby waved her to the back using her confetti shooters like air traffic control wands.

"Did you have a body-oil situation you want to tell me about?" Abby asked after one glance at Lauren's blouse.

"Yeah, my best friend knocked me over with a door, but luckily, someone caught me."

"I don't know, Lauren, it's been a long time since I've wanted to drag a man off to my naughty nook, but I can really picture that redhead in my bed." Abby sighed. "Ah, the benefits of being bi. Truly the best of both worlds."

Lauren had stashed away a pair of binoculars earlier in the day, when she still thought a professional would be in there and they would need a closer look at the details. She found them under her chair and fixed the focus, feet tapping like a nervous rabbit's.

Abby opened the bag of popcorn. "I canceled a date with Anna to stay here tonight."

"The Swede?"

Abby nodded. "That's the one."

"That's why I love you. Not even big boobs and blond braids can get between us," Lauren said.

"Well, that's an image to consider. If you ever want to arrange a sandwiching, let me know."

Outside, the blizzard that had been blowing eased off and plump flakes were drifting down in lazy lines. Inside, though, the Christmas decorations were up, Bing Crosby crooned sweetly, and string lights sparkled.

The lights dimmed and the song changed to "Here Comes

Santa Claus." Abby clasped Lauren's hands. "Here he comes! Please let this work!"

The bellhop wheeled in the giant cake while the knitting society ladies hurried to their seats and started clapping.

"Oh, they put little cat and dog heads as frosting decoration instead of roses, it's so cute!" Lauren said, using the binoculars.

"When does he pop out?"

"Pretty soon, I guess. I told him as soon as the music got funky."

Abby frowned at her. "Funky Christmas music? Surely he'll do it now. He must be cramped in there, don't you think?"

"Oh, yeah. And hot and sweaty…."

Abby choked on a piece of popcorn. "I think it's my turn for a go with the binoculars."

"No, it isn't. My turn just started. Besides, you have two girlfriends!"

"So what? I'm not allowed to admire a hunky man?" Abby snatched at the binoculars.

"Hey, let go!"

"You have to share!"

"No, I don't! This is it! This is it!" Lauren gasped. That roller-coaster feeling of reaching the first hilltop and not knowing whether to yell with excitement or scream in terror took over her body.

It would either be a train-wreck disaster she wouldn't be able to look away from or her saving grace dressed up in faux-leather and body oil. She pressed the binoculars to her eyes. She had to see if the ladies reacted with the same abandon she experienced when pinned to the wall by the bearded ginger.

But mostly she wanted to see Gabe pop out of that cake half-naked and dripping with sweat and frosting. Her mouth watered. Mmm, yeah, to lick that beautiful body clean.

Wait. No. He was Cooper's best friend. There would be no licking.

The lights dimmed further.

Disco spots swirled. The music changed again.

"Is that 'Back Door Santa' playing?" Abby asked. "Oh, these ladies are so bad."

The cake shook.

Nothing.

The two voyeurs clasped each other's hands in nervous anticipation. They held their breath and Lauren wondered if Gabe was suffocating in there.

The cake shook.

Everyone in the room leaned forward.

The top burst off, bits of cardboard, frosting, and sponge cake exploding in an arching spray. A frosting-and-eggnog-oil-streaked Gabe emerged in all his muscular and shapely glory. Rainbow lights from the disco ball swept over him, and stunned silence fell over the crowd.

Gabe did a funky disco move and thrust his hips, winking at his audience.

They went wild, laughing and cheering. While he continued moves that had Abby and Lauren shouting with surprise and laughter, the knitting ladies started to stand and dance too. A couple in the back lifted up phones, taking pictures of each other.

Abby was shaking Lauren silly. "Do you see what I see? Is that the Twist?"

It was indeed the Twist. These ladies were from a different era, and not embarrassed to show it. Gabe escaped the cake and began hamming it up even more, singling out the women who wanted some one-on-one time. Even Ms. Jackson, the stuffy librarian, danced with him—and squeezed his shoulders quite a bit, Lauren noted.

Then the pants came off.

Lauren and Abby squealed in delight. But the ladies had come prepared.

Three of them found their sewing kits and made Gabe stand very still while they stitched his pants together. Santa should seriously consider hiring them as his elves. Lauren wiped at tears of laughter.

Sooner than she realized, thirty minutes had passed and Gabe was waving good-bye, kissing cheeks, and moving toward the exit, leaving a trail of cake crumbs in his wake. Lauren never would have pegged one of Cooper's friends as having so much class.

"I have to admit," Abby said, sighing, "when you said you found some clown to come for free, I was worried. But that man was all kinds of hunkalicious! He didn't do the stuff you usually see, but I would let my arms wrap themselves around him any day! Don't tell either of my girlfriends I said that, though."

"I better go thank him. Hey, we forgot to shoot the confetti guns!" Lauren said, hurrying off.

"I'll save them for New Year's. If you don't need me anymore, I'm outta here, right?"

"Right! I'll see you tomorrow at the bake sale. Drive safely!" The snow might look like an illustration from a fairy tale, but the roads would be hell. Lauren ducked out of the ballroom, scanning the lobby for Gabe.

The clerk at the counter said he had seen a bare-chested man covered in frosting being escorted to the pool showers by the hotel owner's daughter, Shannon, so Lauren waited for him in the changing room.

She had only paced the length three times when a voice warm enough to melt icicles broke the silence. "How was the show?"

"It was…" She whirled and forgot what she wanted to say. "It was quite a show."

Gabe leaned in the doorway, a borrowed robe tied loosely around his hips. His hair was still wet, and the crisp, fresh smell of soap wafted into the room.

She shivered again, trying to shake from her head the image of him wearing only a red thong with a very full pouch. He would be so much better without the thong.

The butterflies in her stomach headed to lower regions, stirring things up that hadn't been stirred in way too long.

He cleared his throat.

"Oh, you need your clothes. I'm sorry, where are my manners? Let me grab my stuff real quick." Lauren babbled on and brushed by him on her way out the door. A pinch in her chest made her pause. So what if he was her brother's friend? She was an adult and could spend time with whomever she wished. "About that drink—would you like to go get one now?"

"I would love to, but I was supposed to meet back up with Cooper when I was done helping you."

"Well, I'm sure we'll see each other again before you leave town," she said. Considering how idiotic she'd been for thinking he was the stripper, she didn't actually believe he would want to see her again. Besides, he was here to party with Cooper, and her brother would certainly introduce him to all the girls he knew. Not to mention the fact that Cooper tried to kill any males who went near her. No, she wouldn't be seeing him again. Not alone, anyway.

All said and done, she was fairly certain he had already forgotten his threat to dare her.

"I'm sure we will." Gabe gave her a knee-bending grin. "And remember, the next dare is mine."

Chapter 3

Lauren sweated the entire drive home. By some strange luck, her car stayed on the road, but only because she kept her speed at ten miles an hour. Gabe's voice haunted her every tortuous minute of the way, promising her a dare.

Cooper wasn't home when Lauren let herself into his townhouse. Her breath continued to plume on her walk through the living room. They could store raw meat on the mantle, it was so cold.

Cursing her brother's weird belief that keeping his place chilly during the day and downright freezing at night would kill germs and boost the immune system, she found a spare blanket and a pair of his sweatpants. Simply adjusting the thermostat when he was gone wasn't an option. No, no, that would be too easy. The space-age device was hooked to Cooper's smartphone for remote control at all times, and he was much too evil to share the access codes while she was a *guest* there, no matter how much she whined for them. Her chattering teeth echoed through the quiet house, and she undressed in Olympic-record time to dive between the icy sheets.

She couldn't believe her mom and stepdad had bailed on her for Christmas. A couple of weeks ago they suddenly informed her they would be gone for the holidays. The announcement came before she'd had a chance to drink her morning coffee, and she hadn't taken it well. Not only were they off for a cruise in the Caribbean, but they had rented out their house to a family of strangers, so she would have to find another place to stay.

"You put out an ad for 'a seaside cottage perfect for a romantic getaway or family fun during the holidays'? What about my seaside cottage for the holidays? Where am I supposed to live for a week?" Lauren asked, peevish.

The choices had been simple: Aunt Jo's and the animal menagerie from hell, or the meat locker. Lauren shivered, thinking of her aunt's place, but it wasn't from cold. Maybe she could deal with the horde of cats, but not the dog.

Her parents had promised her they had worked it out with Cooper. *No problem*, they had said. *You'll have a lovely time, just you and your brother.*

Yes. Lovely. Just me and him. And his nonexistent heater.

What she wouldn't give to snuggle up to a different kind of heater right at that moment. The kind she could rub oil onto. Visions of Gabe popping out of the cake, with his glistening chest and ripped arms started dancing in her head, and she drifted off.

A loud *bang* pulled her from sleep. Burying her frozen nose under the covers, she tried to figure out what had woken her up. Men were laughing in the living room or kitchen. Cooper…and someone else. Gabe?

There was a thought to keep her awake. She moaned, hitching the covers higher and curled in a ball in an effort to warm up. He could keep her warm. If they weren't at her brother's house and she hadn't made such an idiot of herself tonight.

Her feet were popsicles, and the cold seeped through the two layers of blankets and into her whole body.

Temptation would be sleeping just down the hallway from her.

Raucous, obnoxious belly guffaws boomed in the kitchen. Glasses clinked on the counters. So much for sleep.

The clock read midnight. She groaned, covering her ears with her hands. The alarm would go off at six in the morning, and she intended to make just as much noise then as the boys were now.

Wait. How many voices did she hear? It must be three or four plus her brother. Well, he had two sofas and plenty of floor space. Luckily she had claimed the bed before he invited other people home.

Exhaustion lulled her back to sleep as male voices rumbled through the townhouse.

The click of the door opening cut through her slumber.

Weight jostled the mattress and a warm body slid in next to her.

"Whoa, what the—?" She shot straight up, flailing her arms and connecting with someone's nose. A man grunted, yelling a nasally curse like a sailor with a bad cold.

She switched on the lamp.

Gabe was protecting his nose, half-kneeling on the bed.

"What do you think you're doing?" she asked.

"I thought I was getting in bed."

"Not with me, you're not." Despite the fact that he was totally hunky, she didn't know him that well. Fantasies or no, this was reality.

"I didn't know you were in here. When Coop invited me he, said he had a spare room."

"Invited you? To stay at his house?"

"Yeah, for about a week. I told you I had an interview in Richmond this afternoon. Since that's only an hour away…"

She frowned. "That's why you get to sleep in my bed?"

"Cooper told me it was my bed. Scout's honor."

"Tough. It's the sofa for you tonight." It was too late for this nonsense. "I've already claimed the spare bedroom."

"Yeah, except there are already two guys on the sofas and another on the floor with the last blanket. Listen, I'm going. But could you pass me a pillow and one of yours?"

"One of mine, what?" She clutched her blankets to her chest. It was too cold to give one up, even to save someone else from freezing to death.

"One of those," he said, pointing at her fists but meaning her covers.

Uh-uh. "No can do, it's too cold."

"I know it's cold. That's why I'm begging you to please give me one," he said.

"Hmmm. You'd better talk to Cooper about it."

"He's passed out in his room, with only one blanket. He already handed out the extra blankets. You wouldn't be so cruel as to make me sleep with my coat on, would you?"

Could she be that cruel? Maybe.

His lips did that quirked half smile that made her brain chant things like *Kiss, kiss, kiss* and *Whatever he wants, say yes.*

And besides being irresistibly lickable, he had saved her butt tonight. Lauren sighed.

"No, you shouldn't have to sleep in your coat." She peeled back the top layer of blankets. Her hand brushed against his when she gave him the pillow. Tingles quivered in her chest and belly.

She had an extra pillow in hand when she realized she was making another grave mistake. The frigid air was already nipping viciously at her skin, in spite of her long pajamas. She'd have to go find a hat and some wooly socks. She hated sleeping with socks.

Gabe took the pillow and said good night.

"Wait," she blurted out. "I can't let you leave with that blanket. I'm sorry, you'll have to give it back."

"Seems awfully harsh. Sure we can't flip a coin or something, at least?"

"What about going to a hotel? You'll be warmer and more comfortable."

"I can't aff—I can't because I just had two shots of whiskey and put your brother and three of his buddies to bed, all of whom were so drunk I'd hate to leave them alone tonight."

"Let me just…" Lauren crawled from the bed, biting back curses at the pins and needles the cold floor gave her feet. She stormed off to her brother's room, furious he'd put her in this situation, only to find him wrapped in his fuzzy blanket, a pool of drool spreading on his pillow. A quick inspection of the townhouse proved Gabe was right. Snoring, drunk men infested the place.

Maybe they'll make themselves useful and warm it up with their body heat.

Cooper would pay for this fresh hell, starting at 6:00 a.m., sharp. Shoulders slumped, she returned to the spare bedroom.

Gabe lay in bed, both covers spread out and a lump running down the middle.

In the low light of the lamp, his eyes were dark and his form inviting. She had to sternly remind herself they were splitting the bed due to the situation and nothing more. The fizzing warmth spreading between her legs wasn't helping her, though. The memory of him pinning her to the wall and standing shirtless over her brought a hot rush of blood to her cheeks.

He nudged the pillow in the middle of the bed. "Look. My half"—Gabe patted his side—"your half." He patted her side. "You're perfectly safe with me."

That wasn't exactly what she wanted to hear, but with her brother and a bunch of dudes crammed in the house with them, it was probably for the best. Gabe didn't look like the sort to be quiet when he had a woman in his bed.

Then she kicked herself for thinking about him banging headboards into walls. Sucking in a deep breath, she jumped under the covers, teeth chattering.

"You do know Cooper would kill you if he knew you were in here with me, right? Of all the psycho overprotective brothers in this world, he's the worst. I didn't have a boyfriend until he left for college, and only because there was a new guy at school who had never met him."

"But you're an adult now. You can date whomever you want."

She chuckled. He was adorably naïve. "Am I the only one who has met my brother?"

"That bad, huh?" Gabe asked. "Well, I'm not afraid of your brother, just so you know."

"I don't want you to freeze to death, that's why I'm letting you stay in here, but you should know you're risking your life."

"Got it. Honestly I wanted to save this for something else, but given the extreme cold in this house, I'm going to use my dare tonight," Gabe said, a smug quality to his voice.

"Tonight?" Oh God, what was he going to tell her to do? And she was dressed in sweats to do it. The humiliation.

He clicked off the light.

"I dare you to keep your cold hands and feet off my hot body."

***

Despite the whiskey and late hour, Gabe couldn't fall asleep. He was too agitated. Instead, he listened to Lauren's breathing. Within minutes of the light going out, she was asleep, and seconds after that, she lost the dare.

Like little heat-seeking missiles, her feet crossed to his side and zeroed in on his calves. Not long after that, she tossed and turned to his half of the bed and onto his chest in an all-out invasion.

Then he *really* couldn't fall asleep. Why had he wasted his dare in the first place? It had been on the tip of his tongue to dare her for a kiss, but he was already pressuring her into sharing the bed with him. It would have been too much.

No, he couldn't sleep.

Entirely too many distractions. Her silky hair tickling his chin, her hand on his chest, her icy nose pressing against the bare skin of his neck, and her soft curves taunting the length of his body. He was majorly turned on, but not just for a one-night stand or quick tumble in the hay.

He had been looking forward to meeting her for years. Cooper, in his older-brother style, would talk about her both with annoyance and pride.

For some reason, though, Gabe hadn't imagined she would be so damn sexy. His friend had left that out of his descriptions. The soft breasts, the flare of her hips, and her dark eyes. But more than that. She had an contagious energy, an alluring draw. It had gobsmacked him into performing a striptease for a room full of elderly ladies. Not a bad accomplishment for a woman he'd just met.

What he wanted to do with her now was far from how he imagined their first meeting to go—hanging out in a bar with Cooper or having dinner as a group of friends.

He certainly didn't want any groups or her brother around. He wanted her sweaty, panting, and up against the wall.

Yeah. Sleep took quite some time to sneak up on him.

Faint snoring woke him around five. It was surprisingly cute.

Lauren was still curled against his side, stealing more warmth than she gave, but Gabe didn't mind. He lay an arm possessively around her waist, loving how her curves felt against him.

When the alarm buzzed at six, jolting him out of a very pleasant dream, Lauren took several confused minutes to wake up. She stretched and then burrowed deeper into the crook of his body before snapping back. The empty spot she left immediately chilled. In more ways than one. She scooted away when all he wanted was to pull her back in.

"Didn't we have separate halves?" She blinked at him with puffy eyes. She had drooled a bit on his shirt. He loved it when he had that effect on women.

"I moved to the middle. It was a necessary evil to prevent hypothermia," he said. "However, you crossed onto my half with your cold feet first."

"I did not."

"Yes, you did, and then you drooled on my chest. See?" He pointed to his shoulder.

"Oh, that's not embarrassing at all." She groaned softly into her pillow. "It's still freezing in here. You must have tempted me with your body heat. There was supposed to be a pillow."

A few inches of her neck peeked through her brown curls. He almost reached through to see if she was ticklish there. He resisted. "It's not a problem for me, if it's not a problem for you. Since you lost your dare, I'll get another one, though."

"Why don't you dare me now and get it over with?" She

snuggled deeper in the covers, not touching him, but not leaving the bed, either.

"Because the only dares coming to mind now are morally reprehensible."

"How reprehensible? Mildly or shockingly?" She looked up at him. A gleam sparked in her eyes and faint dimples appeared in her cheeks. Oh, he really liked those.

"I would shoot for mild, but it might morph into shocking." He could think of several shocking things to dare her to do, but he was afraid of moving too fast. If he let slip the wrong words, he wouldn't be able to slow down or take them back.

"A mildly morally reprehensible dare that isn't illegal or harmful?"

He propped his head up, lying sideways to face her. With her tousled hair and mussed pajamas, she looked unbearably soft and kissable. *She wants to be dared.*

He fisted his hands out of her range of sight. "How about a dare that is quite a bit less reprehensible than doing a striptease in public?"

She glanced downward and twiddled with her blanket before answering. "That leaves a lot of wiggle room." At least she seemed contrite about it.

"I can't force you to do anything you don't want to do, but…"

"But what?"

"You started this," he said. "I think you want to keep going." *God, let her want to keep going.*

She squirmed slightly, jostling the bed. His hands burned to pull her into his arms so he could attack that creamy, smooth neck with his lips and beard to make her squirm more. For starters, anyway.

"All right, what's the dare?"

"Since you failed so miserably at keeping your hands off me while you slept, then I dare you to put your hands on me now that you're awake."

"You dare me to touch you? Where?" she asked, eyes popping wide open.

"Wherever you want. As little or as much as you like, it's up to you. I let you choose."

"Mildly morally reprehensible? Touching isn't bad."

"Then why are you stalling?"

Her gaze strayed down, scanning the length of his body.

Thankfully, the covers hid his tented pajamas. Just having her looked at him that way sent ripples of desire through his gut to his balls and tighten his erection even more.

"I'm not stalling."

"I dare you to touch me." He had to force himself not to move. It was starting to hurt. "But only if it isn't harmful to you in any way."

"It isn't...it wouldn't be...harmful." She studied his face an eternal moment before brushing her fingers through his beard. Setting every nerve afire. He inhaled sharply, chest expanding.

He kept still while she traced the lines of his jaw and cheek up to his forehead. Each thin trail she created left blazing lines in her wake. It was too little and too much at the same time.

"Wherever I want?" Lauren's breath hitched. She seemed to waver between desire and doubt.

"Wherever you want. I dare you."

"Here?" She slipped her finger under the top of his t-shirt to his collarbone. Fingernails scratched him lightly.

His muscles ached from holding himself still. Visions of pinning her to the bed and doing wicked things to her danced like damn sugarplums in his head. If he knew what the hell sugarplums were. They must be delicious if they tasted anything like he imagined Lauren would. The places he could lick—

He wrenched his focus to the here and now. "I said wherever you want and for however long you want."

"For however long? Did you say that?" she asked with a teasing grin, and her hand came up. She cupped his cheek to rub his lower lip with her thumb. It tickled. He hoped she would never stop. Then again, if she didn't stop, he'd lose the shreds of control he currently had.

He flicked his tongue out for a crumb of a taste, and she gasped. His teeth closed in on her thumb before she could pull away, and he drew it in his mouth.

Her eyelids fluttered. She sat up straighter in the bed, watching his every move but not saying a word.

Running his tongue along the pad of her thumb, he sucked gently, willing her to come closer. When she did lean forward, he couldn't resist the temptation of bare skin between her top and sweatpants. Velvet and cream.

She jolted, sucking in her stomach and glancing downward. "Wait, who's doing what to who here?"

Goose bumps formed on the warm skin under his fingertips.

He freed her thumb from his mouth. "Who's doing what to whom."

"Did you just correct me?"

"More setting the example," he said, running his fingers around to her back and up a few inches of her spine. He wanted to run them down much farther down to the soft curves and dips of her lovely ass. He bit back a groan.

She arched into his touch and the rounded peaks of her hardened nipples pressed at the front of her shirt. He was losing it. And he didn't even know what *it* was.

"So is the dare over?" she asked, voice husky with

emotion.

He hoped the emotion was the same one driving him crazy to touch her with his hands and then his tongue. Although, at the same time would work too. Shifting higher, he leaned forward to plant a row of soft kisses along the base of her neck. "Only when you are tired of me."

"Right." She trailed her fingers to his nape and into his hair, breathing faster.

Gabe reined in his desire to push up onto her and take things to another level. This wasn't a race he could win by going fast. And he intended to win. Instead, he ignored the insistent, tight pain of his erection demanding release and caressed Lauren's side to her hip. Then, slipping his other hand under her waist, he urged her closer.

He guided her, rolling onto his back, until she was straddling him. Heat flowed through her pajama pants to his stomach where she sat. By now, his cock had taken on a life of its own, trying to bust free of his pants. It twitched, knowing Lauren was almost within reach.

She sat straight up, lifting the hem of his t-shirt to touch his torso. His skin jumped and quivered, shocks running from stomach to heart. He mirrored her touch but went farther, the backs of his fingers grazing the undersides of her full breasts. She sucked in her breath, squeezing her thighs around him.

He wanted to memorize every gasp, every shiver, and every hesitant advance she made so he could replay it in his head over and over. This morning was worth savoring, now and later. Her eyes were closed in pleasure and lips parted. He pushed himself up with one hand, feeling her fall slightly against his erection. Ignoring the blind lust that hit him, he moved in for a kiss.

He brushed his lips to the corner of her mouth.

A door banged in the hallway.

Gabe jerked upright, suddenly remembering whose house he was in, but Lauren threw herself backward, terrified. As he reached for her, a mousy scream escaped her throat and she slid off the bed onto the floor, dragging the covers with her.

"Lauren?" He leaned over the edge.

"You cannot be in here. You have to hide. No, I'll go out and distract him, then you sneak into the bathroom or something." She pulled on her pants and hopped free of the blankets at the same time.

"I admit this isn't the best place to be doing this, but we're both adults," Gabe said. "If we're discrete—"

"Discrete? If he finds out you even looked at me sideways, he'll have your balls nailed to the fridge. Discretion won't save you." She motioned for him to follow behind her while she put her ear to the door. "It's clear. When I ask how his evening was, you sneak out and head for the bathroom."

"Lauren, I—"

She ignored him and opened the door cautiously, then tiptoed into the hallway.

Gabe fell back onto the bed with a sigh, rubbing his face in frustration. He had no intention of being afraid of his best friend. Even if he crossed a line he shouldn't with his best friend's sister and his best friend decided to nail his balls to the fridge. Some things were worth the risk.

Chapter 4

A few deep, calming, erection-lowering breaths later, Gabe followed Lauren's path out of the room and down the hall. Her voice reached him loud and clear.

"Yes, I know what time it is. This is when we get up to go to work. If you have a hangover from your evening out, it's not my problem."

By the time he reached the kitchen, Cooper was making coffee, bleary-eyed and hair on end.

He roused himself, squinting at Gabe when he walked in. "Wait a minute, where did you sleep last night? Were you...did you sleep with my sister, man?" His words were garbled as though he had marbles in his mouth. How many drinks did he have before they opened the whiskey? "Because if you touched her, I'll have to kick your ass. Nothing personal."

"Cooper, no, he did not sleep with me," Lauren said.

"We slept in the same bed, yeah," Gabe interrupted, helping himself to a cup of coffee.

"We had an arrangement for him to stay on his half, which he did, like a true gentleman, and there was a pillow in between us." Lauren widened her eyes at him. "By the way, you totally forgot to tell Gabe I'm staying with you through Christmas."

"I told him. I told you, didn't I?" Cooper asked. He pressed his forehead, rubbing.

"No. You didn't. How could you forget to tell him?" Lauren asked, voice shooting up an octave.

He winced, then shrugged. He popped several aspirin into his mouth, then he took sip of coffee to swallow them.

Gabe crossed his arms across his chest, taking in brother and sister in a sweeping gaze. "You forgot to tell me. And another thing, you need to rethink your thermostat. Your sister had her cold feet on me all night, plus around 3:00 a.m. Dexter tried to get in the bed and grope me. I had to take him to the living room and explain a few things."

"Wait, while you were in bed with my sister, Dexter tried to get in bed with her too?"

"He did what?" Lauren asked. "Is this a true story?"

"Good thing I was there. He grabbed my package. I almost punched him, but your sister was glued to me for body heat, and it didn't seem right to wake her up with that sort of violence."

"He grabbed you, thinking you were my sister? Is he still here? I'm gonna kick his ass. Wait, she was glued to you? What happened to the pillow?" Cooper asked, head turning between them so fast his coffee sloshed on his hand.

"Pillows, schmillows! What's this about some other guy sneaking into my room?" She poked her brother's chest. His coffee spilled again and he muttered a curse.

"Who needs a pillow when I'm around to drool on?" Gabe asked.

"Explain this to me slowly." A dangerous glint crept into Cooper's eyes.

Lauren dragged her finger across her throat behind her brother's back, but Gabe simply tipped his coffee cup at her. She huffed and grabbed a cup from the cupboard, slammed the door shut, then banged the metal coffee carafe on the countertop. A chorus of groans billowed from the living room.

"I'll clean if you want to cook us something," Gabe offered from his stool at the counter.

"I don't cook before seven in the morning." She grabbed the milk from the fridge, then slammed that door too.

"Then I'll cook and you can clean. How do you like your eggs?"

"Alone!"

"Lauren, you're killing me," Cooper said, hunching his shoulders at each clang. He collapsed on the other barstool. "Gabe, what the hell happened last night?"

"You invited five friends over, Coop, that's what happened, and you forgot to tell them I was in the spare bedroom."

"I forgot, and there were only four friends. So what happened to the pillow?"

"Lauren got rid of it. Your sister is a big girl, Coop. She knows how to handle herself and get what she wants."

"The hell are you saying?" Cooper smacked his cup down on the counter, eyes focused on Gabe.

"He's saying if you didn't keep your thermostat on fifty degrees at night, I wouldn't have to resort to other sources of warmth to keep from freezing. Even if that source was a stranger crawling in bed with me."

"I'm sorry, but I forgot." Cooper threw his hands up. "I have a lot on my mind these days."

"How long is Gabe staying?"

"Until Christmas Morning when I drive home. I can sleep on the sofa from now on. Oh, and it's a good thing you aren't attracted to me," Gabe said. "Just think of all the terrible things that could have happened."

Cooper stood so fast, his stool rocked and nearly fell. "I don't at all appreciate what you're insinuating."

"You stay out of this, Gabe, I'm having a discussion with my brother." She dumped her coffee in the sink and dropped her cup after it with a clatter. "Your coffee stinks, you know that?"

"Let me make this clear—my sister is off-limits." Cooper turned to Lauren. "All right. I have talked to Gabe, he understands you're off-limits, and I'll talk to Dexter as soon as my head stops hurting. He won't go within a mile of you unescorted, I promise."

"Fine."

"So now that I understand Lauren is off-limits, how about we find some of those hot Sycamore Cove chicks you were telling me about, Coop?"

When Lauren whirled to face Gabe, her finger pointing, he shrugged slightly to ask what she was going to do about it. If she accepted Cooper dictating her life, who was he to fight it?

"I'm going to work now. I'll be home very late and will expect the spare bedroom to be free of intruders." Lauren stalked out.

Gabe couldn't stop staring at her firm ass as she went. He might have copped a quick feel of it during the night. Accidently, of course. He could still feel it in his palm.

Cooper groaned, his head in his hands.

Gabe sat in silence for a few minutes while Lauren pounded through the house with her boots on. The front door banged when she left.

Cooper leaned toward Gabe. "She can overreact sometimes. Nothing happened in there, right? I trust you like a brother."

"No, nothing happened." Gabe swirled the contents of his cup, wishing he could find some sign of the future or tidbit of wisdom in there. The lie rolled out easy but tasted like scum. If Lauren didn't want her brother to know she was attracted to one of his friends who crawled in bed with her last night, then he would respect her wishes. For now.

***

Lauren slammed the door on the way out, gritting her teeth against the blast of cold air whipping her hair and coat around. She stomped through the knee-high snow toward the white mound that should have been her car.

What had started out as a delectable morning, waking in the arms of a green-eyed Greek god, rapidly deteriorated into a total disaster the second real life caught up with her. To top it off, one of Cooper's idiot friends came in during the night and she owed a thank-you to Gabe for sparing her an unpleasant encounter.

But he had practically spilled the beans about their morning together. The whole thing had made her defensive and crabby. She didn't see an end to her running streak of failed romances anytime soon.

At least the snowplow had cleared their street. She was parked at the end of the drive. The one thing she had done correctly in the last twelve hours.

Ice and snow flew off her car in a sparkling spray as she scraped.

Yes, she found Gabe attractive. No, she couldn't let Cooper know about it. He would crucify any guy who tried anything with her, especially one of his friends.

If Gabe wanted to go drinking and picking up chicks tonight, then he was just being true to himself. Knowing firsthand why so many girls fell for him didn't mean she had to continue with what they started. So he made her clothes try to throw themselves on the floor. It didn't matter. He was in town for some fun and she had other plans tonight.

Plans involving pies and furry, little animals.

***

A spicy, cinnamon odor reminding him of Lauren still filled the spare bedroom when Gabe returned.

Tangled blankets littered the floor. Out of habit, he pulled them back in place, tucked in the corners and tossed the pillows on top. He'd much rather get under them with Lauren again, but apparently she was gone for the day and quite possibly not interested any longer.

He had some Christmas shopping to do, and Sycamore Cove was jam-packed with boutiques and tourist stores. That would take half the day. First, he needed to get some breakfast. He checked in his bag for his wallet to see if he should withdraw any cash. Most stores, even the mom-and-pop shops would take credit cards, but it didn't hurt to have a few dollars on hand for coffee.

His wallet wasn't in the bag. He dumped it on the floor to find the jeans he had been wearing last night. Damn. Last night he had taken his clothes off at the hotel. The wallet had to be in the changing room. A flush of heat coursed through him when he remembered taking off his sweater and t-shirt for Lauren and the look in her eyes. Not a good train of thought at this time.

Wallet.

Breakfast.

He grabbed his coat and car keys and headed for his car.

At the desk of the Portside Hotel, he asked if someone had turned in his wallet. Would he be that lucky? He was waiting for the clerk to check the lost and found when the tall brunette who had taken him to the showers at the pool last night came around the corner.

"Mr. Nicholson, so nice to see you again." She placed a well-manicured hand on the counter, close to his. "How can we help you?"

"My wallet has gone missing. I hope you either found it or it's still in the changing room."

The clerk returned, shaking his head. "I'm sorry, sir, but unfortunately it hasn't been turned in."

"Why don't you come with me, Mr. Nicholson?" The woman took a ring of keys and led Gabe to the hallway to open the room for him. "Have a look around. If it's not here, our cleaning lady might have picked it up."

Gabe nodded and went in. A familiar square of leather peeked from under the table. He crouched to retrieve it and saw a white bottle by the table leg. The eggnog body oil. He hoped it would come in handy and picked it up as well. "Got it. Thank you."

"I'm so glad." Every word was drawn out as long as possible.

"You're a real life saver. Sorry to have bothered you."

She partially blocked the exit and only moved sideways a little when he walked out the door. Her heavy perfume filled the air.

Gabe brushed against her thigh on accident.

She smiled. "Mr. Nicholson, you are no bother. I don't suppose I'll see you at the Sunnyvale Retirement Home this evening?"

"No, why would you see me there?"

"I thought you were part of Lauren Hall's fundraising committee. They'll be there tonight selling Christmas crafts and decorations, and I've volunteered to represent the hotel. My father owns it. The hotel, that is, and we support having a new animal shelter go up in town."

"The whole committee will be there?" he asked. "I might drop in for a moment, in that case. To support the cause. Have a nice day, Ms.—"

"Shannon. Call me Shannon. Call me anytime you like." She handed him her card, then strode languorously toward the lobby to show him out. That allowed him ample time to admire her swaying hips and shapely legs, but not a single urge or indecent idea came to him. Nope. Nothing happening down south.

The only urge he felt was an overwhelming one to find the only French restaurant in Sycamore Cove.

Ten minutes later, he pulled his car into the ice-encrusted parking lot behind Les Amis d'Isabelle. The crisp air outside flooded his lungs, and each exhale puffed out a frosty, white plume. A gray winter sky hung low and heavy but did little to dispel the festive feeling in the air and streets. Christmas lights and ribbons decked every corner and doorway in the historic district.

Down the street an open square was filled with cut pine trees being prepared for the tree-decorating contest Cooper had told him about. Apparently, it was a huge deal in the town, but he couldn't quite understand the attraction. In fact, he couldn't figure out why anyone would ever want to live in a little town like this, despite the quaint charm.

Give him a city any day. Richmond was already a stretch, being a small city, but at least the buildings stood over four stories tall. If he got the job, he would only be an hour away from Sycamore Grove. And Lauren.

Not that it mattered. What mattered was getting the job. His savings would only last a couple of months.

This would also be the opportunity he had been searching for to get away from the rut he had been in—endlessly reporting the same sales numbers to his asshat manager. This was his chance to leave the business industry and never look back.

Maybe he wouldn't be making a difference to the world if he worked for the governor. But it would be a start.

The scent of freshly baked bread hovered around the restaurant. A bell chimed his arrival. A woman called out in French, but he had no idea what she said.

Then a smiling, bouncing Lauren came into view. His morning was bright again, and those indecent ideas and urges lying in wait flooded his mind.

"*Bienvenue à Les Amis*, table for...one?" She danced out of reach when he stepped closer, a frown pinching her eyebrows together.

"One, please. What do you recommend for breakfast?" The warm scent of buttery croissants mixed with coffee stirred his stomach to a frenzy and made him salivate more than was socially acceptable.

"Depends on how hungry you are. I can honestly recommend everything on the menu except for the snails, but we don't serve those until noon, anyway."

He followed her to a booth and slid into the seat. The menu went down in front of him, and he took her fingers between his as she turned to leave.

"Lauren, I wanted to tell you—"

"*Un peu de café, monsieur?*" A magnificent woman in her forties stood at his table, platinum-blond hair swept into a loose bun and bright red lips parted. He didn't' understand what she had said, but he could imagine her using the same tone to invite a man for a glass of wine before an open fire.

Lauren pulled her hand free. "Americano coffee, espresso, french press, what would you like?"

The woman smiled warmly at him, too warmly, and her

eyebrows shot up to her hairline. Did she want something from him? An answer, perhaps.

"Yes, coffee. Whatever is in the pot," he said.

She poured him a cup and gave him a tiny carafe of cream.

"*Voilà*," she said, and strolled to the next table, which had recently been vacated.

"I'll let you look at the menu," Lauren said.

"No, wait," Gabe said. "This morning was all wrong. Let me rephrase that. The first part of this morning was great. I've had more fun with you than I've had in a long time, and I'd like for it to continue. Come get a drink with me later."

"You're here to hang out with my brother, and I'm pretty sure you're meeting up with him later."

"Come with us."

"No. I don't hang out with Cooper. He's a schizophrenic serial dater who warns me not to drink or look at boys and then gets the phone number of every hot girl who walks by. You two will have much more fun without me."

Gabe stirred his cream into the coffee but kept his eyes on her. She was lovely in her frilly apron and pale blue shirt. Her tight-set jaw told him not to compliment her on it. "Why are you so angry this morning? Is it because of Cooper?"

"I think for someone who breezed into my life less than twenty-four hours ago, you really don't know me well enough for this conversation."

"Do you remember how you acted yesterday? Who you were during those few minutes when you were simply Lauren and I was just the kitten-loving, male dancer you dragged into a closet? And then this morning, before you remembered he was home and we might get caught?" He didn't know her very well, but he had known her for six years through her brother. Gabe was fairly sure Cooper was the crux of the problem. She was afraid of her brother's reaction.

She drummed her knuckles on his table. "Yesterday I thought you were a professional getting ready for a job, and this morning was big mistake. I can't get involved with one of my brother's friends."

"But you liked getting involved with me. I could see it," he said. "We have fun together. Take us in the bed last night, for example. I mean, you couldn't keep your hands off me."

"Feet, Gabe. I couldn't keep my feet off you."

"True, but then this morning after one little dare your hands were all over my body."

Dishes clattered, startling them both.

The French woman stopped cleaning the other booth and nodded at them. Her eyebrows would mate with her hair if they went any farther up. "Keep going, this is a very good story. Really, don't mind me."

"Isabelle!"

"It has been so long since you've had a man, *chérie*. Tell me you two did more than just touch. I've said before, too much suppressing your libido is unhealthy."

"Isabelle, I know this is your restaurant, but could I have a moment alone, please?"

The owner sighed and walked off, shaking her head.

"Gabe, whatever might have happened is never going to happen," Lauren said. "I don't need a guy who is in town for a few days to keep me warm for a night or two, and you don't need to ruin your friendship with Cooper. That's all there is to it."

"That's not all there is. Don't worry about any repercussions on my part with your brother. You need to live your life without him dictating what you can and can't do."

"Not happening. This little game is over. What would you like to order?"

Chapter 5

Lauren drove straight from work to the Sunnyvale Retirement Home, her trunk full of the fresh pies Isabelle and the cook had prepared. It was their contribution to her fundraiser for the animal shelter.

In fact, Isabelle was the person who had tipped Lauren off to the poor conditions the animals were living in after she took home a little Papillon puppy. According to Isabelle, the building smelled like rot, water stains covered the ceiling and the kennels were older than the Paris catacombs. Plus, it was too crowded since the staff were all darlings who never refused an animal or enforced the rule of putting animals down if they were elderly or not adopted fast enough. Maybe the shelter wasn't horrible enough for it to be shut down, but when Lauren called to offer her help, the receptionist started crying with gratitude.

The cafeteria at the retirement home was decked out Hallmark style in holiday cheer. Besides the tables decorated with ornaments and candles, over a dozen tables groaned under the weight of baked goods and knickknacks for sale.

Stringed lights colored the room, holly and mistletoe hung in every doorway, and Christmas carols completed the ambiance.

She pushed the door open with her hip and strode in, juggling five boxes stacked one on top of another and calling out hellos. The craft and bake sale was finally on. Too bad she was carrying so many pies, she could have done a quick jig. Maybe she'd do one later.

The event would only bring pocket change to the cause, but it was vital for community awareness and support. Approaching the retirement home had been her idea—they had more than enough unused land surrounding their building, and more than enough residents who loved animals.

Building a new shelter next door to them would be a wonderful solution to several problems. Senior citizens could volunteer to care for animals who needed attention, and animals could provide companionship to elderly people struggling with loneliness and depression. Not to mention the families who visited their loved ones would be parking right next to the shelter as well. It would be a win-win situation if she could pull it off.

Lauren was in the process of putting the finishing touches on her table when she heard a woman's throaty laughter. "Mr. Nicholson, what a pleasant surprise."

Nicholson?

Why did that ring a bell? Someone from the mayor's office? She looked up toward Shannon's DJ stand.

Gabe. Gabe Nicholson was chatting it up with Shannon. She handed him a contest form to fill out. As if he needed to win a prize in order to have a free night at the hotel her father owned. From the way she leered at him, she would find him a room and put herself in it the second he snapped his fingers.

Jealous much, Lauren?

She rolled her shoulders and adjusted each of Isabelle's

pies a few centimeters left or right to be more aesthetically appealing. *I'm not jealous. That's ridiculous.*

But why was he here?

The second the thought flitted through her head she felt like an idiot. He was here to see Shannon. They met at the hotel last night. She showed Gabe to the hotel pool showers and gave him a bathrobe to wear. Which was probably more comfortable than the man-thong Lauren had given him.

He must have gotten Shannon's phone number at some point.

Before or after he dared me to touch him wherever I wanted?

Jealously was not a pretty emotion, and Lauren hated herself for feeling it. After all, Gabe asked her to go out for drinks when he came to the restaurant this morning and she had turned him down. Was the man supposed to become a monk simply because she didn't want him?

He was in town for a good time. Shannon would certainly be happy to provide it.

Lauren kept her back to the talking couple until Shannon laughed particularly loudly. Giving in to her flight instincts, she pretended to go check on the other stands in the opposite direction.

Handmade soap, Christmas wreaths and tree ornaments, pop-up cards, heavenly smelling organic coffee. She almost stopped for some but then heard Gabe's voice coming closer. Lauren crossed the cafeteria and plunged through the swinging kitchen doors. Dinner was finished and the place was scrubbed clean.

Lauren paused to peer through the crack between the doors, only to see Shannon steering Gabe toward the kitchen. She shut herself in the storage pantry just as they came through the swinging doors. As she swallowed her anger and tried to find a place to sit, Shannon guided Gabe into the pantry, joining her.

She scoffed under her breath. He didn't even wait a whole day before getting it on with the next woman in line.

The metal shelving in the storage pantry made a terrible cover. Lauren scooted behind a tower of Buckworth's Best Breading, letting loose a silent string of expletives. Her plan to avoid the couple had backfired spectacularly. She dropped her heavy head into her hands and imagined herself on a tropical beach.

Seconds later, Gabe was pressed into a corner while Shannon wrapped herself around him octopus-style.

"This certainly is a well-organized establishment," he said. "So what about that—"

"Tell me more about your college days with Cooper," Shannon purred. Actually purred. "You know we went to high school together, but he was a year older, so we never hung out. What was the craziest thing you two did?"

Lauren put a hand over her mouth to stop from groaning.

"There were a few wild parties we crashed. You?" He resembled a buck with a prize pair of antlers caught in a hunter's sights.

Lauren almost felt sorry for him, except he wasn't trying that hard to escape. He was a player through and through. One woman in the morning, another in the evening.

"There was this time two of my sorority sisters and I climbed to the top of the Pi Kappa Phi's house to moon everyone after a football game. The cops showed up right as we were in the middle of things, and we had to run off without our panties!"

"I bet that was quite a sight. So when did you say—?"

"You bet it was a sight. And it still is, if you're curious." Shannon moved Gabe's hand to her ass, a glint of *come and get 'em* in her eyes.

This was really not how Lauren envisioned spending her evening.

Shannon helped Gabe squeeze her backside. "Maybe it's time to get familiar with it."

And...cue my exit.

Gabe coughed. "Here in the pantry?"

Grabbing a bucket of breading to hide her face, Lauren stood to go.

"Don't mind me," she yelled.

Gabe and Shannon jumped and a half a dozen cans crashed and rolled on the floor.

"I just had to come in here and get some of these amazing bread crumbs. I've heard they're the tastiest thing to happen to chicken since pot pie!"

Lauren pushed by the stunned couple and was halfway to freedom when Gabe took the bucket.

"Lauren, I was looking for you. Let me help you with that. Shannon, it was great meeting you. See you around later, perhaps with Cooper some time, all right?" he said, following Lauren into the huge kitchen.

He stayed on her heels as she wove through the maze of countertops and ovens.

"Hey, slow down," Gabe said. "I'd like to thank you for saving me from the facehugger back there. Not that I usually mind a woman who knows what she wants, but since I came to find you—"

"I didn't save you," Lauren said, rounding on him. "I saved me. There are some things in this world I would hate to see."

"Me too." He leaned on the bucket he had set on her table and surveyed the layout. "Speaking of pie, are these yours? I've heard stories but never believed them."

"What are you talking about?"

"Your pie, Lauren. It's legendary."

"My pie? I have no idea what you're talking about."

"I've been dying for a taste since I met you." He winked.

"You did not just wink at me. How much have you had to drink?"

"I did just wink at you. I haven't been drinking. Don't believe me if you want, but stories are told in hushed, reverent voices by teenage boys at Eagle Scout campfires about a woman in Sycamore Cove with pie to die for."

She glared at him, hoping his beard would frost over. "Thirty seconds ago, you were one inch away from exchanging buccal fluids with Shannon in a pantry and now you are talking dirty to me."

"Is there a question in there?"

"No—yes. Why are you here?"

"Second time in two days a woman has pulled me into a closet. That's a new record for me. But that's not why I'm here."

"I pulled you into a closet for a legitimate reason."

"And it's the same reason I came tonight. There are kittens to save, and I want to do my part by buying one of your pies."

"Cooper already bought one. If there are any left over, you can buy it later," she said, dismissing him with a wave.

"I also came to see you," he said, not moving from her stand.

"I thought my brother made it clear that I'm off-limits, Gabe. And why aren't you with him tonight? Weren't you supposed to go to a bar and pick up chicks?"

"Your brother had a thing to take care of, and besides, I'd rather be with you."

"Listen, you two won't be friends anymore if he finds out we were in bed and about to...you know...things were happening." She fidgeted with the tablecloth. Why did he make this so hard? All he wanted was some quick action while he was in town, and everyone would be better off if he did it with someone else. Like Shannon.

Jealously pricked her stomach. It wasn't something she wanted to imagine. She'd rather picture a beach and piña coladas.

"Yeah, about that, I would appreciate it if you stopped worrying about my life. Worry about yours and ask yourself why you let your brother make decisions for you. I came because I wanted to be with you tonight."

"Is that so?" Her hand moved to her face before she caught herself. Their almost kiss on the bed burned at the corner of her mouth. His lips had barely brushed hers, but now that she remembered, it felt like a brand.

"Yes." He moved in closer, drowning her in his warm scent and tall strength. His green eyes darkened and a faint smile line on his cheek appeared.

"You'd rather be here helping me with the fundraiser than drinking with Cooper?"

He frowned, a question in his expression. "Helping with the fundraiser? How, if I'm not allowed to buy a pie?"

"By doing what you do best. Making women feel loved. Holding them tight in your arms and showering them with affection. Making them feel like they are the only woman in the world, until the next one comes along, of course."

He frowned deeper. "Do I have to go in the closet again?"

Lauren refused to laugh, although her lips twitched with a smile. She looked pointedly across the wide room, past several stands to an evergreen arch covered in fake snow. "Wait here for a moment."

The man setting up the arch was a sweet, nerdy college student who happened to have a terrible crush on her. She had never encouraged his fumbling advances or awkward silences, but tonight she would use his puppy love to her advantage.

"Hey, Stanley, how's it going? Getting things ready?"

He jolted to attention and mumbled about how ready everything was and how excited he was to be there.

"Could you possibly do me a big favor? Bob could really use an assistant at the change-and-payments table. Plus, my brother's friend is visiting from out of town, and he would love to lend us a hand. I don't trust him with numbers and cash like I trust you, so I thought he could take your place and you could help Bob. How about it?" It was a stretch, but she was counting on him not asking too many questions.

"Oh, yeah, I could do that. And your brother's friend can just do this."

"Thanks, you're great. I'll send him over," she said with a clap to Stanley's shoulder, buddy fashion.

He stumbled over his own feet in his rush to do what she asked. In some other life, she would take him aside and try to teach him how to kiss girls, but not in this life and certainly not when Gabe was around. Not that she would be kissing him tonight, either. His only goal was to get laid and she wasn't falling for his charms.

The almost kiss flared to life on her skin, and she pressed the spot with cool fingers. Gabe thought her brother controlled her every decision? Hardly.

She assumed a triumphant stance and returned to her pie stand.

"You want to help? Then you can man the *hugs* stand for me."

"I'm not buying baked goods and Christmas knickknacks?"

"Afraid of a little work, are you?"

"No," he said. "You know I'm not afraid."

But he was hesitating. Something was holding him back.

Lauren could sense it.

Too bad. The cafeteria had a disproportionate number of females coming in, especially older women. He would make a killing in this crowd, which meant more money for her project. Lauren leaned forward, crooking her finger at him to meet her halfway across the table.

"I dare you. I dare you to go over there and give hugs until the lights go out. I dare you to prove you care about something besides yourself."

His eyes sparked with sudden fire. "Do you? You know I'll dare you back."

"Do your worst. I'm not afraid. I. Dare. You."

The transformation from indecision to action was immediate. He stood up straight and pulled off his sweater in one smooth motion and then crowded into her personal space. His snug, black tee showed off his wide chest and shoulders, and exposed his sculpted forearms. Women would flock to his snow-covered pine-bough arch in droves. She would be strong and abstain. Somehow.

"Game on," he said, so close she could see the individual flecks of gold and green in his eyes.

She repressed a shiver.

"And you'll stay there for as long as you have a line of ladies needing affection," she called as he strode off to the arch. His whole body projected masculine confidence, as though he already knew he would raise a ton of money for her. Goofy, lovable Stanley didn't hold a candle to this Adonis.

Abby arrived in time to see him lifting the sign that read "'Hugs $1 each,'" and rushed over to Lauren, bearing a steaming cup of coffee.

"Is that our cake man giving hugs?" she asked, voice thick with admiration.

"Yes, it is," Lauren answered. That had been ridiculously

easy. She'd spoken the magic words '*I dare you*' and he'd torn off his sweater and ran to get under the arch.

"Like a fairy-tale gingerbread man you want to nibble on," Abby said under her breath. "I wonder how much money I have in my bank account..."

"If I thought you had any money, I'd let you keep him nice and busy. As it is, you'd better get to work." Lauren turned her attention to her table. The doors were officially open for the sale. Families and individuals trickled in for their Christmas goodies fix.

Isabelle had prepared a delectable selection of pies and cakes ranging from typical American to traditional French. Lauren was sorely tempted to buy one or two, but she had to save her money to buy hugs later.

As she thought of those hugs, her gaze flickered toward Gabe. He had fallen right into her trap.

Lauren could see that everything was a game to him, and the only way to win was playing down and dirty. All is fair in love and war, *n'est-ce pas?*

Oh yeah.

Admittedly she was a tad nervous about his next dare, but in a spine-tingling, panty-melting sort of way. She had willingly put herself in trouble again, after so narrowly avoiding it this morning. Those broad shoulders and cut arm muscles would be her undoing, sooner or later. Probably sooner.

On the other hand, he was doing exactly what she wanted—staying busy raising money for her project.

He chose that moment to glance over and smile. His first victim toddled up with her walker.

Get hugging, buster.

He stooped over and gently wrapped his rippling arms around the blue-haired, fragile woman. He held her for a long moment while she patted his shoulder and hip.

Oh. Whoa.

Who knew he would be so lusciously sexy holding the elderly? She had painted him as a one-night junkie, but she couldn't deny he was a mouthwatering distraction.

Maybe he was more.

She shook herself mentally and bestowed her warmest smile on the people approaching her stand. Time to work. The local news channel for their county would be in later for an interview. The fundraiser needed corporate support and probably some big donations from the wealthy in order to get to the halfway mark.

Handing out dollar bills to elderly women for hugs (to keep Sexy Gingerbread Man busy until she was ready to leave) would be the perfect ending to the evening. It would be heartbreaking for Gabe not to have any work and leave the bake sale early.

Chapter 6

Whatever Gabe had imagined selling hugs at a small-town fundraiser in a retirement home would be like, he was wrong. Dead wrong.

It was so much more fun.

Things started sweet and innocent, but that didn't last. Hugs were a dollar a piece, and ladies young and old came by, chatted a moment, and then bought their hugs.

The local news sent a journalist and a small TV crew to do a report on Lauren's project. Gabe listened in while the woman described the deplorable conditions for animals in the current shelter and why a new one should go up on the land near the Sunnyvale Retirement Home.

Lauren shone like a beacon, her cherry lips smiling, and glossy chestnut hair begging for his hands.

Chestnut hair? When had he started using words like that? He snapped out of his daze to the strains of "Chestnuts Roasting on an Open Fire."

Shannon, managing the music table, winked when he looked her way. She held up a finger for him to wait.

Wait for what? Wait…wait…

"Up on the Housetop" piped through the speakers. He swallowed a groan. How could he make it clear he didn't care to see her bare ass mooning him from a rooftop or anywhere else?

While the journalist, a young black woman whose name was Sandra if he heard correctly, was going around doing her interviews, his line for hugs slowed to a trickle. This gave him time to watch as Lauren walked around the cafeteria, introducing her fundraising committee and enticing Sandra to sample the goodies.

They were at the booth next to his, admiring sparkly baubles as Lauren explained something, letting her hands do most of the talking. If it was in his nature, he would have been jealous. There she was, up to her eyebrows in her dream. Gabe relaxed on the edge of his table, waiting. No one seemed to notice him at his deserted hugs stand.

Until someone handed him a kitten in one hand and a puppy in the other, and shoved him into the limelight.

Sandra saw Gabe first, her face lighting up at the sight of the furry babies. "Aw, Lauren, look at this. Are these animals from the shelter?"

Lauren, however, wasn't cooing or gushing at all. She froze, eyes wide. "I don't…why, yes," she said, looking over Gabe's shoulder. Someone must have been prompting her. "Yes, the wonderful volunteers from the shelter brought a few animals over to see if anyone would adopt them tonight. Apparently, this kitten and the…dog…puppy dog don't have homes, so if anyone out there wants to give them a family…" She tried to back away slowly, but the crowd and the cameraman propelled her forward, vying for a better view.

"They are so sweet!" Sandra air-kissed them in rapid fire. "Let's get some close-ups."

The animals were squirming out of Gabe's hands by that point. He needed help. The nearest person not holding anything was Lauren, so it seemed only natural to give her the puppy, since the cat was climbing up his chest.

The puppy whined and wriggled and jumped from his hands. For a second, he thought she would watch the puppy fall.

She squeaked, catching it at the last moment. Then she held it as far from her body as possible, mouth opening and closing but no words coming out. Face ashen, she scanned the crowd as though searching for something.

Was she afraid of the five-pound pup trying to lick both her hands clean simultaneously? Because that would be absurd. She thrust the puppy at him for him to take it back.

Another young woman shoved her way through and plucked the brown-and-white ball of energy from Lauren's hands, saying she would take him over to the information desk for adoption. Before Gabe could blink again, Lauren was smiling and chatting. It was as though nothing had happened.

A mic was shoved in his face and the journalist holding it motioned for her team to move in closer.

He squinted into the dazzling lights, and the kitten succeeded in scaling his chest.

"And what is your name, sir?" Sandra asked.

Gabe smiled for the camera, reaching up to keep ahold of the black kitten perched on his shoulder. The tiny thing batted at the tinsel draped around his neck, its claws digging into his skin. He clenched his muscles to keep from showing discomfort.

Sandra's dark brown eyes swiveled to his bicep, and she was no longer addressing him but his arm. Awkward.

"Gabe," he said, coughing to cover up the fact that he didn't say his last name. "I'm helping out tonight and I sincerely hope somebody will take this kitten home. Right this minute, in fact."

"Oh, isn't that adorable?" Sandra asked his arm. The leggy journalist sidled closer to him. Wide, pink lips smiled at his muscles.

"Yes, it is."

"Do you come with the kitten? A package deal?"

"Ah, no, I'm simply manning the hugs station. Hugs are only one dollar. Buy as many as you like."

"Really? That sounds like a deal I might need to take advantage of." She took a last, lingering look at his arm and faced the camera. "Well, there you have it, folks. Hurry down for a lovely time. Adopt a kitten, donate for a hug, or buy a pie. Anything and everything you contribute will go toward building an entirely new shelter, which would have a no-kill policy and be located right here with a beautiful lawn and wonderful people all around it. Thank you."

The crowd dispersed, and Gabe spotted Lauren weaving through the onlookers.

"Wait," he said. "Are you all right?"

"I'm fine. Why do you ask?"

"For a second there, it just seemed like..."

"Gabe, I'm fine, and you've got a line forming," she said. "See you later. Much later."

After that, things got warmer and very hands-on for Gabe. The kitten effect? The close-up of his bicep on TV? He didn't know, but more and more women lined up for hugs, and not just quick squeezes.

They wanted full-body cuddles and weren't afraid to cop a feel of his buns too.

In fact, several women returned quite a few times. His feet and back ached from standing and bending over so long. Lauren flicked into view, going from table to table talking to groups of elderly women. He gave another hug, this one a cheek-to-cheeker.

When he told her good-bye, a flood of women who had been busy at bingo got up and trotted over, waving dollar bills and flashing false teeth at him. Lauren was nowhere to be seen. What had she said to them?

These octo- and nonagenarians were insatiable. One even invited him back to her room for a lesson in "knitting." Air quotes were supplied by the speaker.

He noticed many of his customers were also part of the knitting society he had danced with the evening before. At this rate, he'd be there until midnight, while several of the crafts tables were already closing up shop.

Shannon came by several times, adding to his line.

"How much longer does this stay open?" he asked Shannon, who was clinging to him for her third hug.

"Not much longer. Already have something planned?"

"Yeah, I do. I'm supposed to meet up with my friend in town. It's a guy thing."

She sniffed. Was she smelling him or expressing doubt? "Well, let me know if you need any company. There are some great spots I'd love to show you while you're here."

"Will do." There was a break in his line. This was his chance to escape for a few minutes at least. He scanned the area for Lauren, but her table was clear and she wasn't in the cafeteria.

He said good-bye to Shannon, then interrupted a group of fundraiser workers chatting nearby. "Excuse me, has anyone seen Lauren? With the brown hair?" He motioned to show he was searching for someone fairly short.

A skinny guy looked at him askance as soon as he said her name. "She's in the kitchen straightening up. Do you want me to get her?"

"That won't be necessary, thanks."

The man continued to glare at him.

"I'm her brother's friend and just would like to give her a…thing." Gabe edged around the group toward the kitchen. The other man kept watching him. Small-town mentality was strange.

Under the suspicious eyes of the fundraiser guy, Gabe found the "thing" he wanted to give Lauren a couple of tables over. Paying, he held it low and to his side to hide it from view.

Still no Lauren in the cafeteria. He headed for the kitchen, checking left and right to be sure no one else was going that way. Once inside, he saw her puttering around with plasticware in the back.

She was alone. Perfect.

"Lauren," he said, walking resolutely up to her and taking her arm, "it's time for your dare." He pointed with his chin for her to march.

"What? Right now? What are you hiding?"

"Yes, right now. You'll find out. Is anyone in the pantry?" It was time someone dragged *her* into a closet.

"I don't think so. Are you hoping to meet up with Shannon again?" Her words tumbled out fast and glib.

She was nervous. Good.

"Get inside. Now."

"Is that my dare?"

"No. That's so we'll have privacy during the dare. You want privacy for this one, believe me."

"Wha—?" she sputtered as Gabe led her inside and closed the door behind them. "So you've heard just how good Buckworth's Best Breading is, too, and you want your own bucket?"

"Don't you think it's funny how many women wanted

hugs, especially several hugs tonight? Almost as if there was a cosmic conspiracy to keep me too busy to do anything else."

"You aren't complaining about your success, are you? All the money you raised goes straight to this project." She crossed her arms.

"Whatever your plan was to keep me away from you, it didn't work. Now here's your dare." He slowly pressed her into the corner, leaning down until her hair tickled his lips. "I dare you to close your eyes, open your mouth—"

She laughed. "And I'll get a very big surprise? What is this?"

"I wasn't finished," he said, lowering his voice to a warning tone. "Close your eyes, open your mouth, and get on your knees."

Her plump, cherry lips rounded in an 'O,' shocked. "You can't be serious. Kneel?"

"I. Dare. You. Mouth open, eyes closed, and on your knees."

"Here in the pantry?" Her chest rose and fell rapidly and she fidgeted, each movement bringing them in contact.

"It's the closest thing to a closet as I could find." He shrugged. "As for what will happen, I'm pretty sure it's not illegal, but don't quote me on that, and it's not harmful if you hold still, and I don't think either of us is too worried about morals." He stepped back to give her space. "Do I have to double dare you?"

"No, I…on my knees," she said, voice catching.

He could actually feel her gaze heating up his skin as it traveled downward at the same time she lowered herself to the floor. Hands fluttered to his legs to steady herself.

"Good. Mouth open and eyes closed."

She swallowed and then did as he ordered.

By then, his erection was raging in his jeans, driving him

insane. Lauren was beautiful in the half-shadows of the cramped pantry, kneeling in front of him.

She was willing to take anything he gave her. And why shouldn't he take advantage of such an offer? Bending low, he grasped her hair at her nape and held on firmly.

"Careful now, this is going to get very hot." He paused, considering what he was about to do. "And foamy."

She whimpered in anticipation, tilting her head closer to the sound of his voice and curling her fingers on his legs. *Hot* wasn't the word. She set him on fire.

He took her surprise from behind his back and slowly pressed it against her lower lip. Then he changed the angle of his hold so a few drops spilled on her tongue.

Lauren gasped, her eyes flying open. "Coffee? It's coffee. I can't believe you."

"Eyes closed," Gabe said, pouring in some more.

She moaned in appreciation. "It's from the organic stand, isn't it? Oh God, it's so delicious."

He couldn't take it any longer. He lifted the cup away, then he brought his lips down on hers for a coffee, cream, and cinnamon kiss that seared through his chest and rocked him to his soul. His senses sped into overdrive, sending messages his brain wasn't able to process. All but one—Lauren's soft lips were under his.

She moved with him, testing him and tasting him. Her breath whispered into his mouth and he pulled her closer. One hand cupped her head, deep in her hair, the other hand slid downward with a will of its own to her shoulder blade and spine. It ran up and down, eliciting a thrilling shudder from Lauren. Her tongue danced over his as she melted into his arms.

To hell with meeting up with Cooper. What did he have to offer compared to Lauren? Cheap liquor in a smelly bar.

No, he wanted to kiss Lauren senseless all night. And in the morning, wake up by her side and spend another day making her laugh. Or making her beg. Or both.

She fit with him, her softness, her curves, and he breathed her in, needing more. He'd only met her yesterday, but he couldn't imagine letting her go. He tightened his hold.

Spend the rest of his time in Sycamore Cove lost in coffee kisses with this amazing woman? Hell yes.

Hell...no.

No.

This wasn't in his plans. He refused to get into anything more than a good time.

Lauren waited in his arms, lips parted and eyes closed.

And Gabe stood and left while he still could.

***

Reeling from the hottest kiss of her life, Lauren swallowed, savoring the coffee-and-Gabe taste lingering on her tongue. After a few moments of silence, she blinked her eyes open. Apparently he wasn't coming back for more.

He had left her on her knees and alone in the pantry. Alone. On her knees. Which had begun to ache.

Standing on weak legs, she took stock of the situation. Once again, she had let him get too close and have too much. All he had to do was focus those emerald eyes on her and smile to make her do his bidding. When he told her to get on her knees and open her mouth, she did it without a second thought.

Heat flared in both her face and darkest nether regions, leaving her confused as to whether she was embarrassed about degrading herself or angry he ran off the second things heated up.

That kiss.

She replayed it in her mind. His lips covering hers in fierce urgency, his tongue lashing into her mouth and then out again, his hands in her hair keeping her powerless, and the rough scratch of his beard. She rubbed her lips lightly, recalling the pressure and moisture.

For a girl who had decided she wouldn't have a relationship, casual or other, with one of her brother's friends, she was certainly in constant danger of taking off her clothes. If Gabe had dared her to strip, she would have.

Someone banged the cupboards in the kitchen, and Lauren hurried to straighten her hair and shirt, then stepped out of the pantry as innocently as possible.

It was Stanley, finishing up with the plasticware. "Your brother's friend was looking for you. He said he had to give you something. Did you see him?"

"My brother's...yes. He gave me a...a coffee. It was hot. And foamy. And I left it in the pantry."

They stared at each other in strained silence as several seconds ticked by. Lauren did an about-turn and returned to fetch the forgotten coffee from the floor. Stanley hurried off.

On her way out of the kitchen, Abby swooped in, and grabbed her arm.

"Have you seen the cake man recently?" she asked but didn't wait for an answer. "Check him out and tell me if you've ever seen anyone yummier."

In a Santa hat, Gabe reached to the top of his booth's arch to fix a crooked decoration. His t-shirt hem lifted with his arms, showing six-pack squares and part of his V. Lauren's knees threatened to buckle.

"Yeah," Abby said. "Spank me, Santa, because I've been a naughty, naughty girl."

"Abby, it's all an act. No one is that sexy and smart and considerate and actually donates time to save animals." The kiss had been part of the game to him. Nothing more.

"But he can still spank me, right?" Abby asked. "Because you have to admit, the only thing missing on that package is a ribbon."

"I'm calling it an evening. Thanks, sweetie, for coming in tonight."

"My pleasure," Abby said, giving her a big hug. "You're set up for the boat show. I won't see you for a couple of days."

"That's right."

Lauren didn't know if she wanted to party it up with the sexy Santa or hide in a corner and cry. She was bushed after a full day's work at the restaurant and then several hours at the sale. Every part of her body ached. Feet, calves, back, shoulders, and the bruise in her chest Gabe had caused. And Gabe could either heal it or tear her chest wide open. He might do both.

Her hands trembled as she buttoned her coat. This was ridiculous. What she needed was a good night's sleep.

At least the pies had all sold, leaving the one Cooper bought under the table. She deposited her money with Bob at the bank table, then made a goodbye round, thanking everyone for their work.

She even thanked Shannon for taking care of the music, noting how the other woman seemed self-conscious around her. Embarrassed about the pantry? She should be. Of course she didn't know about the second time Gabe was in there.

The cafeteria was nearly empty except for a thinning crowd around the hug stand. Lauren knocked her knuckles on a table for luck that this project would work. She would never raise the one million necessary to build the facility, but if she could raise public awareness and enough funds to push the mayor's office into action, then he would finish what she started. Abandoned animals from in and around the town would have spacious cages, clean floors, outdoor play and exercise areas, and a covered walk between the shelter and the home.

Too good to be true?

Gabe laughed with the elderly woman he was hugging.

Sexy, smart, successful, considerate, fun, and interested in her? Nothing was ever that good.

He said something in the woman's ear and she laughed too. Devilish thoughts about dragging him into the pantry made Lauren's cheeks hot. The things they could do together. A very different sort of ache throbbed deep in her body. It was time to admit the truth.

She had it bad for her brother's friend.

Chapter 7

Gabe had it bad for his friend's sister. Very, very bad.

He came to Sycamore Cove for fun and parties, nothing more.

At some point, Lauren started leading him around on strings, getting him to work for her project, and the second he had a chance to get what he wanted in return, he lost his self-control. Wanted more than her lips on his.

Kissing her while she knelt in front of him stirred up a whole shitstorm of emotions he didn't want to deal with.

His nature wasn't to ignore the sort of advances Shannon made simply for a kiss from Lauren. He should have gotten more or nothing at all.

He was a dumbass, but luckily this variety of stupidity had a cure. Get drunk and have fun with a girl, any girl, including Lauren herself. Get it—whatever it was—and the girl out of his system.

He called Cooper. It went to voice mail after several rings. He hung up, annoyed. His friend was having one problem after another between his start-up business and some woman messing with his head. He had mentioned a Sandra. As in the journalist?

Gabe had to chuckle. From the smoldering looks she had given his arm during the interview, she was either the wrong Sandra or she didn't give a rat's ass for Cooper.

But that wasn't Gabe's problem. His problem was that Cooper had zero time for partying. This visit was turning into a bust. A waste of time.

It seemed like the perfect plan. Fly to Richmond for the interview at the governor's office, then drive to Sycamore Cove to see his friend for the first time in a year. With a little luck he would know if he got the job in a day or two. But until then, he'd spend his time finding chicks and kicking back in bars.

Not...fundraising.

After offering to take down the arch and turning over the money he had raised, Gabe braved the icy outdoors, rolling his shoulders to loosen the tension and get heat in his body. Stinging snowflakes attacked every exposed inch of skin, and he blinked them from his eyes.

The parking lot was dark and mostly deserted. Lauren was sitting in her car, though, letting it idle to warm up. Through the patchy darkness, her interior light shone on her head. Just a pretty girl. He could find a dozen others as attractive in every town in America. Why waste time and risk a good friendship on her?

She glanced up, perhaps sensing she was being watched.

When she saw him near the building, she didn't smile or invite him closer in any way. In fact, she seemed surprised he was there, curious. This would be a good moment to set things straight by telling her he didn't need or expect anything from her.

A few quick steps brought him to her door, and she rolled

down the window.

"Are you lost?" she asked.

"No. About the pantry, it was just a dare, a game. But we're even now. It was fun hanging out with you, and I hope you change your mind about coming out for drinks with your brother and me. The three of us could have a good time."

"Just a dare? A game? You think you can get out of the next dare that easily?"

"I was thinking we could call it a win-win situation. You have been worried about Cooper finding out and him trying to...what was it? Nail my balls to the fridge? Which would be very unpleasant, I have to admit."

"So you are afraid of my brother." She shook her head. "Every guy is, sooner or later."

"I'm ending this game because *you* are afraid of your brother." It was close enough to use as an excuse. He wasn't up for dealing with complications. Or emotions. Definitely no emotions.

"And if I told you we could keep it casual during your stay in town? That we could have a little fun before you go and then pretend it never happened?"

That was certainly an interesting proposition. Not something you heard every day. "What sort of fun do you have in mind exactly?"

"The next dare is mine. I'll have to see what I can come up with." She rubbed her gloved hands together. A corner of her mouth twitched to smile a couple of times.

"I'm only around until the twenty-fifth. Christmas Morning I'm flying back to Boston."

"Yeah, you mentioned that this morning. That means we only have about three days. What do you say? Cooper doesn't need to know what doesn't concern him." She spoke so quietly, he had to lean closer, much closer, to hear. He crossed his arms on her car door.

Ignoring the fast punches hitting his ribs, he nodded. Knowing she wanted to stay casual before things went further took the danger of falling for her. Since she didn't want more, he wouldn't give it to her.

"Why don't I get a hotel room?" He could dip into his funds for a good cause. "That is, if that's what you have in mind when you say fun. Because that's exactly what I mean by fun."

She hesitated. She stopped rubbed her hands and tucked them under her thighs. Breaking eye contact, she gnawed her lower lip before answering. "Not right away. Cooper would be suspicious, I think. Besides, until after the Christmas Tree Decorating Festival, there won't be any open rooms."

"I think I could find one if I looked hard enough." He could always ask Shannon for a favor, right?

Her head snapped around. "If you look too hard, you won't need to invite me."

"I'm joking. If you want to wait, that's fine. But don't wait too long."

He brushed her hair from her shoulders to reach her nape and draw her in to him. Her cold nose tickled his beard and cheek and he pressed his lips to hers as a delicate seal to the agreement. Nothing set in concrete, no emotions.

Then her tongue flicked across his lips and he leaned farther in, deepening his kiss. The same searing burn from before moved up through his chest. He grabbed the handle—

Swerving headlights flooded the car from behind and someone honked.

"Hey!" Cooper shouted. "Get away from the car right now, asshole!"

Lauren hissed in surprise, throwing her head into the seat, but Gabe stood slowly, waving. "It's me, dickhead, just checking the temperature readings on her dashboard. Not much of a car for the snow."

"Oh, hey, what's up? I thought you were some prick bugging my sister." Cooper slammed his door and crunched across the slick parking lot to hit Gabe's shoulder in greeting. "There's my little sis. How was the bake sale? Where's my pie from Isabelle, my French mistress?"

"You wish she was your mistress. It's in my trunk," Lauren said, jerking her thumb toward the back of the car.

"I wish? She wishes. She asks me out every time I set foot in there. So where are we going tonight?"

"I'm going home," Lauren said, emphasizing and drawing out each word. She tapped her fingers on the steering wheel, not looking at Gabe.

"Yeah, I'm ready to call it a day too. Why don't you go on and meet up with the others?" he said to Cooper.

"Screw that. You're buying. I'll call Dexter and John and tell them to meet us at the Broad Street Jazz Club. Can you leave my pie on the counter at the house? You're a doll," Cooper said, throwing his arm around Gabe's shoulders.

The sound of Lauren's car driving off faded, and Gabe resigned himself to an evening of crass jokes and a smelly bar.

***

Her bedroom was lonely and cold that night, but at least she had three blankets and a clean pair of sweats. She curled around her largest pillow, recalling the feeling of waking up in Gabe's arms that morning and kicking herself for not agreeing to rent a hotel room. Not only would Gabe be buck naked and wild in it, she could adjust the heat.

The alarm clock woke her up way too early, and she stumbled down the hall toward the kitchen on her morning quest for coffee. Gabe was in the living room, fast asleep on the sofa, his head buried in the blankets and his back to the world. Damn, he looked yummy.

He tossed to his side and she scurried away.

She was sipping her coffee when her brother appeared like something off the set of *The Walking Dead*. He needed a shave, a shower, and several painkillers minimum to return to the land of the living.

"Why do you drink so much if the next day you regret it?" she asked, handing him his favorite mug. Their mom had sent her a message that morning asking how they were doing and if it was cold and snowy. The Caribbean was gorgeously sunny apparently, and she felt a teensy bit guilty for leaving her two children to fend for themselves in the icy weather.

Teensy was the actual word she used in her text. *Feeling a teensy bit guilty.* Lauren was tempted to take a selfie of herself wrapped in a hoodie and a bathrobe plus a scarf while her mug steamed like crazy, and standing next to her brother with his monumental hangover and unwashed hair.

We're doing great, Mom! Just a teensy bit frozen and slovenly!

"It was fun while we were doing it. You wouldn't believe the mess my life is right now," Cooper said and groaned.

"I might believe you if you told me about it." After all, he was her brother. She already knew about the trouble he was capable of getting himself into. "What's wrong?"

"Work and stuff, you know?" He leaned on the counter in a way that said work was the least of his problems. What the hell was going on with him?

"What kind of stuff?"

He rubbed his face but didn't answer. "Thanks for the coffee, and tell Isabelle her apple pie is *mair vai you*."

"*Merveilleux*," Lauren corrected him. His pseudo-French was atrocious.

"We'll see you tonight?" He slugged back his coffee and

put the cup in the sink.

"I don't know, are you doing something with Gabe?" For once she didn't have any fundraiser or restaurant work. She had been hoping to sneak off somewhere with the redheaded hottie. Alone.

She twisted the life from a dishcloth waiting for his answer.

"Yeah, all the guys are going out to eat at the new Mexican place. You should come, they've got the best salsa."

Lauren had a weakness for spicy food, but the idea of sitting at a table of Cooper's friends and not having a second alone with Gabe was horrible.

"Thanks, but no thanks." She was running late. It took twenty minutes, plus all of her courage, to get out of the semi-warm bed at 6:00 a.m.

Cooper headed to his room to get ready, and Gabe was still sleeping when she tiptoed past him to get dressed. She paused by the sofa, listening to him breathe and wondered if she had any courage left to wake him up. What would she say?

Hey, hot stuff. How's the head? Still looking forward to getting your next dare? I don't know what it will be yet, but it's sure to be a doozy.

She stood there, stupidly, bundled to the eyebrows like a tourist in Alaska.

Sure, she could come up with a dare, just as soon as she thought of a good one. And if not, that was what the Internet was for. Information. Or there were the things he had dared her to do. She could tell him to touch her bare skin, get on his knees, close his eyes, and oh, criminy.

Not possible. She was on a path leading straight to Gabe's bed and her feet were frozen to the floor.

Well, on a path to the sofa. Yeah, maybe they better get a hotel room. Images of being held in his embrace and the moist touch of his mouth running over her skin sent waves of feverish heat through her stomach and into that lonely spot between her legs. She could picture him naked on a bed all too well—the squares of his abs lined up, and his V drawing the eye lower to the ginger hairs at the level of his hips. Lauren moving over him, lowering her mouth to trail down his stomach, readying a dare in her mind—

Gabe stirred and a squeak escaped her throat. She dashed off to her room before he could see her in her wintertime, bag-lady attire.

A few minutes later, she left the house through the garage, avoiding the living room and the kitchen. She was beginning to regret her offer. She was the one who was the total scaredy-cat. She couldn't play games like this, planning on having no-strings-attached monkey sex.

Good thing she would have the house to herself after work that evening. It would be nice to have some peace and quiet for some serious reflection. Maybe she should get her thoughts in order and write him a letter explaining this had been a mistake.

At work, she told Isabelle her brother loved the apple crumble she had made for him.

Isabelle tapped the silverware roll on the table and pursed her lips at Lauren. "Of course he did. It's one of my pies. And the redhead? Anything you want to tell me about him?"

Anything, like she went down on her knees in a pantry when he told her to? "Nope," Lauren said, shaking her head. "Nothing to report."

"Hmmm. *J'y crois rien*," Isabelle muttered. She obviously didn't believe Lauren.

And to think, she had loved every second of Gabe's dare. Maybe instead of writing a letter, she should just go for it. A sexual adventure was new territory for her. What did she have to be afraid of? Gabe was a normal person and not a psycho.

He enjoyed games, so this was certainly something he could lead her into, and he was leaving in a few days. She didn't have to be afraid of bumping into him or seeing him with other women later.

Stop being a chickenshit and just go for it.

She would see him again tomorrow, and she had every intention of telling him to find a hotel room.

The workday crept by slow as icicles forming on the eaves. But as she left to get in her car, the twinkling lights in the town square called to her. Window shopping was all she could afford, and despite her cold toes and constant yawning, she spent a half hour drooling at the lovely things behind the glass.

Thank goodness Cooper and Gabe were out for the evening. She could curl up on the sofa in sweats and watch something that required tissues.

Snow had been piling up endlessly during the day, coming down in huge chunks, and was now two feet deep. She drove at a glacial pace, terrified of sliding into a ditch or the rear end of another car. Her little Honda was not built for winter, but she arrived safe and sound. She should have asked for winter tires from her mom. What had she been thinking to ask for a donation in her name to the fund?

The second she walked inside, dragging gusts of wind and a flurry of snow with her, she dropped her purse, bags of presents, and her coat on the floor. Collapsing back into the door, she yelled, "Yes, yes, yes! Oh thank you, God!"

Christmas under normal circumstances was hectic enough, but add the snow and fundraiser work on top and this year might be the death of her.

A wry chuckle sounded from the kitchen, and Gabe appeared, carrying a bottle of wine.

"No need to thank me. I'm ready for my dare when you are, though."

Chapter 8

Nervous excitement electroshocked her heart. Lauren wasn't ready. She might not be ready for several days. Maybe weeks. What could she possibly dare him to do? She didn't have any kinky accessories packed in her bags, no whipped cream in the fridge, or unusual fetishes he could act out for her. Most importantly, however, she didn't have the guts to dare him to pin her to the wall and kiss her until she melted in his arms and lost capacity for rational thought.

That, and she had no idea when Cooper would be home.

"Would you like a glass of wine now or with dinner? Did you eat? I was about to put on water for some pasta, but don't expect anything fancy. Store-bought sauce and some basic salad fixings is all I found."

"Salad and pasta? Probably my groceries I bought anyway. Yes. I'll have some wine," she rambled. "So where's Cooper? Will he be eating with us?" She pushed free from the door and removed her huge, snow-covered boots. Stepping over the puddles to find a towel, she almost knocked into Gabe.

He smiled down at her and took her elbow to hold her

upright. "He has a thing again tonight. He apologized profusely and assured me several times he won't be coming home, but that we can party tomorrow."

"Not coming home…all night?" she asked, somewhere between incredulous and hopeful. Her brother sleeping elsewhere? The no-commitments womanizer who didn't practice the walk of shame because staying the night gave girls the wrong ideas?

"If I'm not mistaken, he's found someone to get serious about." Gabe ran his fingers up her arm and to her back, sending fluttering tingles through her chest. "It's just us tonight."

"And you have wine?" Lauren would need whatever help she could get in order to dare him. Half a bottle should about do it.

"I also hacked the codes on his thermostat. You may notice you don't see your breath when you talk. Have a seat. I'll bring you a glass and get the food started."

At this rate, he would be wiping Lauren up off the floor along with the melted snow. Dinner, wine, and a warm room. Instead of driving safely home, she'd died and gone to heaven.

"Lauren?" he asked.

She hadn't budged.

His fingers found her nape, and her skin quivered.

"Yes?"

"Do you want to eat? Because if you don't, I'm going to start unbuttoning your shirt."

She didn't answer. She couldn't.

Trailing his hand across her neck and down the bare skin above her collar, Gabe reached the top of her shirt and undid one button. Her heart fisted and then raced, taking her lungs with it.

"After that, I can't make any promises except that I'll be

relentlessly exploring every single inch of your body."

"Oh wow." Her head spun from too much oxygen. He was so sure of himself while she was a clueless ninny. For one weird second, she wished Cooper would come home early and save her from having to decide what to do. She banished the thought from her head. "We better eat first. I'm starving."

They had all night. No rush.

He sighed. "As you wish."

She followed him to the kitchen and sat at the bar while he poured her a glass of wine. They talked about family and work while he cooked, keeping their hands off one another and the subjects safe. He didn't push any more, but he was always close, his gaze catching hers, following her.

After dinner they curled up on the sofa. Her head hummed faintly from the wine, and in the low lights, the room swayed gently. He was close enough for her to smell warm cologne and something spicy—eggnog. A bit of the edible oil must have spilled on his clothes, and it reminded her that she'd wanted to lick him clean the night at the hotel. A flush crept up her neck and cheeks.

"I can't believe this snow," she said. The bottle of wine was nearly empty, and Gabe distributed the last few drops between their glasses. "It must be up to three feet by now."

It was late. Pale porchlights from along the street reflected from the white mass, proving there was indeed a ton of snow outside. Heavy flakes continued to fall.

He drained his glass and agreed with her. Then he laid his hand on her thigh, too high up to be purely friendly. "I'm still waiting for my dare, you know."

"I know," she said, staring at his hand. He moved closer.

"If you don't dare me, then I'll have no choice but to assume your dare is for me to strip your clothes off and get on my knees in front of you."

"Shit," she muttered, picturing him kneeling between her legs, "that would be a good dare."

"It would be a good way to start things off." Gabe brushed his lips against her earlobe. "I understand it's difficult coming up with a dare for me. You've certainly never been around a man whose body is as hot and overwhelmingly sexual as mine. You can't resist me. You shouldn't even try. Confession time. I have wanted you since I first saw you. I know you want me bad because I'm a stud. You are absolutely weak and out of control for me. So either dare me or take off your clothes."

What the—?

She twisted around and stared at him openmouthed for a heartbeat. A satisfied smirk was pasted across his face. What the actual hell?

***

Gabe kept his expression neutral as Lauren stood up abruptly, set her wineglass on the side table, and stormed down the hallway to her room.

Then he grinned. It had worked. Despite the fact she seemed pissed as hell, Gabe calculated it would take Lauren less than two minutes to change her mind and come back to the sofa. She had been breathing fast, licking her lips, and stealing glances at him all evening, sending clear signals that she wanted him.

He'd had to go out of his way to stir her up, though. Sure, the signals had been clear, but she was more nervous than a china shop owner during an earthquake, and who wanted action like that? In less than two minutes, she would be back and ready to go down in a blaze of glory.

He wanted her fire and heat, and Lauren had it in her somewhere.

Sure enough, he heard her rummaging around in the back bedroom, and a minute later she was coming back. She had a strange bundle in her hands. Were those goggles?

"I have a dare. Since your body is so hot, I dare you to go snow swimming."

He laughed. The sparks in her eyes were definitely what he had in mind, but the direction she was headed in was a surprise. "You want me to suffer, is that it? I was joking earlier when I said all that stuff."

"And you're hoping I'm joking now?"

"It's freezing outside." He motioned toward the frosted window.

"But you're so hot, it shouldn't be a problem."

"I don't have any snow pants or a ski jacket," he said, pretending he didn't see the swim trunks and goggles dangling loosely at her side.

"You don't need snow pants or boots for this dare. In fact, you don't need much of anything at all." She put both hands on the sofa back, closing the distance between them.

"Why's that?"

"Because swimming in the snow calls for swim gear. One good dive in, and then you can get out."

"Does my head have to go in, or can I be a chicken and keep it up?"

"Your head can stay up," she said. "Or you can do it German style—you get to soak in super-hot water first, but then you have to run out buck naked and put your head in. I'll let you choose. Either way works for me."

"What if it's so cold I get a heart attack and die, and you feel guilty and miserable the rest of your life?" Although with the heat burning through his core to his skin, Gabe wasn't worried about the cold. A few inches were all that separated them. One quick move on his part and she would be straddling him. A few more moves and he'd have her shirt off.

"I'm willing to take the risk that a quick plunge in the snow won't kill you. So?"

"It could cause an injury."

"Gabe, I dare you."

"No."

"I double dare you, in that case," she said.

How far could he go? She was so unbelievably foxy when he pushed her boundaries. Her tongue flicked over her lips, and her eyes searched his for weakness as she leaned over him.

He placed his hands on her hips. "Still no. It's not a fair dare according to our rules."

"I think fleeting physical discomfort is quite fair compared to going on my knees for your surprise in the pantry." She put her knees on either side of his legs, as if to prove a point. His erection was killing him. He'd never be able to put on swim trunks. "I double-dog dare you."

"I think the dare I proposed was much better." He kissed the skin under her ear.

She moaned, rolling her hips. But that didn't do the trick. "I triple dare you."

"And how will I get warmed up afterward?"

"You'll think of something."

"You want me in swim trunks in the snow? Really?"

"I. Triple. Dog. Dare. You. And you can choose swim trunks or naked. I'm sure the neighbors aren't watching out the windows."

"You...triple-dog dare me?" This was good. This hadn't happened since the fifth grade and he was triple-dog dared to climb the schoolyard fence during recess.

Lauren nodded.

He gently pushed her off the sofa and stood. Her gaze went straight to his pants, where his cock strained at his zipper. He stretched upright, not trying to hide anything, and deliberately undid his belt and button. The temperature in the room shot up twenty degrees.

She stepped back to watch the show.

***

Lauren couldn't quite believe the size of Gabe's…ego. So hot she couldn't resist him? Too weak to control herself? He'd said he had been joking, but she wasn't so sure. Her only course of action was to show him how well she could resist.

Watching him slowly strip in the half-light of a table lamp and the moon from outside tested every ounce of her willpower. Okay. Maybe she was seriously weak for this man. Chiseled cheeks, a square jaw, rough ginger beard, and well-defined, corded muscles would be tough for anyone to resist.

When he reached for his boxers, she cleared her throat and tossed him the trunks and goggles. Then, looking away, she said, "Have you decided to cover your amazing attributes or go in the buff?"

"Since I don't want you or any of the neighbors hurting yourselves, I'll put on the trunks. Do I need the goggles?"

"Only if you are afraid your eyeballs will freeze."

"All right, Lauren, let's do this."

She tiptoed after him to the doorway leading to the backyard, keeping her hands behind her back so as to not accidently squeeze his tight buns. They appeared rock-solid.

He opened the door and wound his arms to warm them up, then took several deep breaths. She snuck past him to the edge of the entryway.

Damn, it was frosty out there.

"Good thing the cold can't touch you," she said.

Gabe grinned, goggles giving him an alien-lifeform appearance. "I feel rather sorry for all the snow I'm going to melt. It only fell a little while ago."

The chill from the floor attacked her bare feet. She hated to think how much colder it was outside in the ice and three feet of snow. "Remember, whole-body immersion, except for face and head. You can keep your hair dry because I'm nice like that."

"I'll keep it in mind for the next dare. All right," he said, preparing for his jump.

"Wait." Lauren grabbed his arm to stop him and he turned, hope in his expression.

Faint traces of his warm, spicy scent teased her nose. She had to squash the voice that started chanting, *Lick, lick, lick.* She could resist his studliness.

He swallowed, towering over her. His arm was tense under her hand, and his erection pushed a clear bulge in his fitted trunks. But the dare was on. She had no intentions of making this easy for him.

"Turn out the lights," she told him. "Just in case the neighbors are up."

He flicked the switch. Lights in the living room and back porch went off, leaving them in the glow of moonlight reflected from the snow.

"Triple-dog dare, huh?" He stepped outside and assumed a diver's position. His muscles popped, and his ass was worthy of being immortalized in a Michelangelo sculpture. She had meant to be cruel. But she was the one suddenly in agony.

He launched his body far over the snow and landed with a *ploof* in the fluffy stuff.

Laughter burst from her mouth before she could rein it in and he muttered obscenities at the snow, thrashing about to stand. "Goddamm, that's cold," he shouted. He was hip-deep in snow, and he pointed his finger at her. "Your turn. Start swimming."

"My turn what? That's like a tag back. Not happening!"

"You didn't call, 'No dare-backs.' Get out of your clothes and into a suit if you have one, and start swimming."

"You're crazy," she said, shaking her head. "I'm not going in there."

"Yes, you are." He waded through the great drift, coming straight for her. With a gasp, she turned to run.

She reached the sofa. Iron arms hoisted her into the air. He lifted her over his shoulder to carry her. "I dare you, Lauren, and if I have to I'll take it all the way to triple-dog dare, the same as you did. Clothes off, now."

Chapter 9

Lauren kicked to be put down at the doorway, and she pushed him aside. He couldn't manhandle her and make her do the same dare. But he was right about the no-dare-back rule. They hadn't specified. Fine. If he wanted to play, she'd show him she could play with the best of them.

She sucked in her gut and unbuttoned her slacks, already shivering. Her nipples tightened. No, they were already tight from the second he grabbed her, and now his heated gaze made them ache painfully.

He crossed his arms, waiting. She tore off her clothes down to panties and tank top before she lost her courage. "Same thing? I can keep my head dry?"

"Wait," Gabe grabbed her arm the same as she had done, and she turned, hoping he had changed his mind. "Shirt."

"But my bra is see-through."

He swallowed, his gaze drifting downward to where her nipples practically poked through the thin fabric of her camisole. It was like a physical caress. She could feel them devouring her. "You can go and get a different one. Or you could tie your tank in a knot," he said, voice rough.

"Screw it." On impulse, she pulled off her top, letting him get a glimpse of what he was missing by making her jump in the snow. Because, yeah, no way was she going to bed with a man who made her snow swim. The faint light in the room was enough to show the expression on his face change from hungry to dangerous.

Too bad. He had dared her to do this. Now she was going to do it, and he could admire the view from afar.

With a deep breath, she hollered a Tarzan cry and ran straight into the massive drifts. She took two lumbering steps in the freezing snow and belly-flopped.

Spikes of cold jabbed into her entire front side. Laughing and screaming, she rolled over to get the other side. The neighboring houses were dark, which meant the people inside were either already sleeping or out. Or possibly watching from the windows, attracted by the ruckus. Just as long as no one reported the spectacle to her brother.

Gabe was holding on to the doorframe, laughing his ass off.

"Oh my God, this sucks so bad," she yelled. Despite having jumped already, he didn't have nearly enough snow on him.

He shook with laughter. "You should see yourself! I can't—"

A snowball splatting on his face shut him up. He yelled something incomprehensible, shaking it off and lunging for her.

She threw another snowball but missed. Dodging his hands, she raced for the door.

Strong arms caught her around the middle and lifted her up. "You're freezing!" He held her like a bride despite her kicking and flailing and started to carry her toward the house.

His hands covered too much of her wet, naked skin.

She was acutely aware of every bit of skin on skin, the rise and fall of his chest, and the strength in his arms keeping her off the snow.

She shivered uncontrollably.

"We'd better get you warmed up," he said, gravel in his voice. They reached the porch.

"Gabe?"

"What?" His breath was ragged with exertion—or something else.

"You're such a dickhead, did you know that?" She had one last surprise for him. Before he knew what was coming, she rubbed her last snowball on his bare chest.

He gasped. "Shi—"

She cut him off with kiss.

The handful of snow needled her skin when she pressed against him, but the warmth of his lips was intoxicating. A split second passed and he grazed her teeth with his tongue. She let him in deeper. She wanted more of him, filling her. He switched his hold to bring her upright, and explored her mouth.

She wrapped her legs around his waist. Biting and sucking at his lips, she kissed him with all the hunger he had shown earlier. Desire spread like wildfire, burning through her body. He carried her inside, knocking the door open and then kicking it shut again.

Her hands fisted his hair, clutched at his shoulders. He held her secure with one arm, while his free hand roamed over her skin, raising shiver-bumps wherever it went. He found her breast and teased the nipple through the sheer lace, pulling a moan from Lauren's throat.

She needed him badly. Judging by the pressure of his erection pushing against her ass, he was ready to give her what she wanted. Small noises she didn't recognize as her own came out of her mouth.

He carried her to the bedroom and tossed her on the bed. She stared up at him, chest heaving for air, and legs slightly apart. He crept closer.

That's right. Keep coming.

He crawled to her, inch by inch, and she reached for him, wanting to feel his hard chest and warm skin covering her.

Leaning down, he ran kisses from her neck to her collarbones and chest and then pulled her bra down to take her nipple between his teeth. Flashes of pleasure rippled through her, sending moisture to her panties.

She gasped, arching backward. Her legs went around his hips and she pulled him flush against her. His skin was hot to the touch despite their romp in the snow. The ridge of his erection pressed into her sex, and she rolled her hips into him.

He ran his fingers through her hair, breath ragged in her ears. He hooked his finger in her pink panties and began to slide them downward. Too much, too fast.

"Gabe?"

"No more snowballs, I'm begging you." He lifted her hips to pull her panties over her round buttocks and down her legs.

"Wait, we can't," she said hoarsely.

***

Gabe paused.

"We can if you want. I have a condom." He stopped trailing kisses past her belly button and lifted his head for her answer.

She was panting and shivering, caught between desire and doubt. Her hands moved through his hair, grasping and releasing.

He kissed her hipbone lightly and moved his hand

between her legs. Her velvety sex was wet, and she trembled under his touch.

"Tell me to stop," he said, slipping one finger inside her. "Tell me to stop now if that's what you want."

"I want..." Her eyes glazed over and her head fell back.

He continued to move inside her in a slow back-and-forth motion and dipped his head for a taste of her. Blinding desire clutched his gut, and he had to force himself to keep the pace slow.

Gabe swirled his tongue on her clit and she gave a small cry.

Moving with her bucking hips, he listened with satisfaction as her breathing grew ragged. He savored her body, testing ways to make her cry out. He wanted those gasps and shivers.

Her hands hit the mattress and she pushed her hips up against him. He moved his tongue inside her. Judging by her soft pleading, he knew an orgasm wasn't far.

The garage door rumbled to life across the hall.

"Shit," he muttered.

Lauren twisted away with a squeal, searching for her panties on the floor and telling him he had to get out.

"Pants! Where are your pants?"

"Living room?" he asked, curses for his friend running through his head.

"Throw these on." She tossed him a pair of sweats, probably Cooper's. They would go great with Cooper's swim trunks that he was already wearing. He pulled them on and pocketed the goggles, grateful his erection had fallen instantly at the noises from the garage.

"Our clothes!" Lauren dashed out of the room to get the things they had scattered on the living room floor, and he reluctantly jogged after her.

Lauren was in her undies and t-shirt, but he didn't have

time to admire the view of her ass waving in the air while she picked up discarded clothes. He grabbed his pants and shirt, then stuffed them under his pile of blankets, then scooped up the wineglasses and bottle to take them to the kitchen. He had time to rinse one glass and put it back in the cupboard before the door to the hallway snicked open. Another door somewhere else clicked shut. The sound of water running and several thumps came from the bathroom.

He walked calmly to the living room to get a t-shirt from his bag, acting as though he was getting ready for the evening and nothing interesting had transpired. If Cooper didn't decide to go back out, the falling snow would even out the holes he and Lauren had made during their near-naked romp. But tomorrow…tomorrow he was getting a hotel room.

"Hey, didn't expect to see you here," Cooper said, walking in.

"Same goes for you. I thought you were gone all night." Gabe leaned on the wall in what he hoped was a casual "I didn't dare your little sister to strip and jump in the snow, then throw her on the bed and go down on her" way.

"Yeah, well. I need some whiskey. You?"

"I'm good. I found a bottle of wine to go with my spaghetti." Gabe followed his dejected friend to the kitchen, surveying the area for any incriminating evidence of an evening with Lauren.

Cooper poured himself a generous glass and skipped adding ice or water. He tossed half of it back and grimaced.

"Wanna talk about it?" Gabe asked.

"Not really. I saw Lauren's car. She's home?"

"She got back a little while ago. I think she's in the bathroom."

"So what about you? I thought you were getting busy tonight," Cooper said.

From the corner of his eye, Gabe saw Lauren appear at the kitchen doorway. She crossed her arms and stopped to listen.

"Yeah, well, no. Not really. I mean, I didn't have anything planned."

"You said you met a hottie who couldn't get enough of you and tonight was the night," Cooper said. "That's why you didn't mind me canceling."

"No, uh…Did I say that?" he asked, nodding at Lauren for Cooper's benefit. "Either of you want some spaghetti?"

"I'm good," Lauren said. "Tell us about this hottie. Do I know her?"

"He told me he met her at your hotel fundraiser thing, the one with the knitting ladies, and then she was there again for the bake sale." Cooper finished off his whisked, then wiped his face with the back of his hand.

"Don't do that. It's uncouth." Lauren threw him a hand towel. "I should know who it is. What else did he say?"

Gabe wanted to punch him.

"Said she couldn't control herself and this was turning out to be the best vacation since spring break our junior year. Right, Gabe? So what's her name?"

"I think we've talked enough about me," Gabe said, neck and face muscles clenching.

Cooper shook his head. "One last thing besides she's smoking hot. He has it on good authority that she needs a man. So what do you think, Lauren? Can you tell me who it is?"

"Let's see: smoking hot, needs a man, can't control herself, and was supposed to be a sure thing tonight. Does that sum up how you described this woman to my brother, Gabe?"

"I'm not talking to either of you." Murderous thoughts stampeded through his head. Guys didn't rat each other out to girls.

"I think it could be either Abby or Shannon Zimmerman. You know, from the Portside Hotel?"

"Shannon Zimmerman? Yeah, she's hot," Cooper said ruefully, gazing at his empty glass. "Although, if Abby brought along a girlfriend or two, I wouldn't say no, personally."

"Do you two hear yourselves talking about women?" Lauren smacked the countertop.

"I hear myself," Cooper said. "What about it?"

"All right, I'm out of here. See you in the morning," Gabe caught Lauren's eye as he left, trying to make her understand he wanted to talk, but she glared at him until he gave up.

He collapsed on the sofa, heaving a sigh of defeat.

Cooper said good night and vanished into his bedroom.

Chainsaw. Axe. Buried alive in the desert up to his chin. One day, Cooper would pay.

"So sorry you didn't get any action tonight," Lauren said as she went through the living room. "Maybe you'll still get lucky, though. Shannon is only a phone call away, if you're feeling lonely."

"You know I'm not interested in her. That stuff I said to your brother was just to keep him from feeling guilty for stranding me. I really wanted him to be busy elsewhere tonight."

"Speaking of getting busy and chicks, maybe you should be interested in Shannon. I'm not sure why, but I think she's into you." She flicked off the light, leaving him alone in the shadows with only the moonlight as company.

Chapter 10

Sneaking out of the house at 6:30 a.m. with no coffee and three feet of snow in the driveway was no easy feat. But Lauren managed.

Not wanting to confront Gabe or Cooper was a great motivator. She tiptoed out the front door, stealing only a quick glance at a sleeping Gabe, wrapped in two blankets and a sleeping bag on the sofa. It had been a cold night for both of them. The other major downside of her brother's impromptu return was his readjustment of the thermostat.

Bleary-eyed and with nerves rubbed raw, she scraped layers and layers of snow and ice off her car, started the engine, and inched out of the driveway. She made it five minutes down the road, which was only five minutes away by foot at the speed she was driving, before her cheap all-weather tires betrayed her. She turned the wheel one way, but the car went the other.

"Dammit, dammit, dammit!"

Her stomach lurched as she slid into the ditch, and she cringed at the hideous crunch when she hit bottom. The roads had been cleared of most of the snow, but black ice and treacherous sludge coated them.

She pressed her forehead to the steering wheel.

She could walk to the house and go back to bed, call a tow truck and wait in the house, or sit there in the freezing car, fogging up the windows while she cried like an idiot for almost sleeping with an egotistical, hot jerk and figure out how the hell she would pay for car repairs and food if she couldn't get to work that morning.

She banged her head against the wheel.

Of course, she didn't have any insurance for this sort of thing. She had a brother who was friends with nearly every guy in town, and he always found someone to bail her out.

A red Ford sedan sidled up beside her. Speak of the devil.

She rolled down her window, wiping at her eyes and nose.

"Hey, what happened?" Cooper asked, leaning far across the front dash.

"What's it look like? Do you know anyone who can come get me out?"

"I think Matt or Trevor might know someone. A morning like this, though, it will take them forever to get here."

"Can you give me a ride, then? I have to get to work. I need my tips for gas and there's nothing to eat at your place." She got out of the car and crawled up the ditch, nearly slipping on the ice.

"Why don't I ask Gabe to take you?"

"No, not Gabe. He's your friend, not mine." Anyone but him.

"You guys get along great. You'll see, he'll be thrilled to save a damsel in distress." He lifted his phone to his ear. "Hey, man, did I wake you? Sorry. Lauren is stuck outside on the road and needs a ride to work, and it's on the other side of town from my office. Yeah? Cool. She's waiting for you."

"Cooper, I hate you sometimes," she said. "Actually I hate you quite often."

He grinned. "You couldn't survive without me taking care of you. How's your fundraiser going? You never told me about the cake thing, or the retirement-home gig. Did Gabe take care things for you? He do all right?"

"Oh, he did all right. Got a little carried away there toward the end with the tinsel, but other than that, he was good."

"Great. I wish I could have seen him in action. You took pictures, right?"

"I think I have pictures. I'll send you something embarrassing if possible," Lauren said.

"He's the only friend I trust around you, you know that?"

"Because he'd never try to get in my panties?" she asked, remembering only too well the moment Gabe had started taking them off. She had never ached so badly for a man before. She had wanted him hard and fast, with no thoughts or worries about the next day.

"That's right. He'd never touch you. He knows better. Which is good, because after all the girls he screwed in college, I wouldn't trust him not to cheat on you. Then I'd have to kill him, of course. All right, I can't get ahold of anyone now, but I'll call around from the office to get your car pulled out of the ditch. See you tonight?" He rolled up his window and waved good-bye before she could answer.

...all the girls he screwed in college. He wouldn't be faithful as a boyfriend. Well, she didn't want him as a boyfriend, so technically that shouldn't matter. She began the slow trudge back to the house, wishing she had boots with cleats or at least a waterproof pair. And a tropical island she could call her own.

Her teeth chattered and her hands were red and numb by the time she reached the driveway at the house. Gabe stepped out onto the porch, coat unbuttoned, no gloves and hair scraggly. She wanted to run her fingers through it.

"I was just on my way to get you. Did you have to walk far?"

"Good morning," she replied, making a beeline for his rental instead of going for his hair.

"Good morning," he said with a smile.

He got in on the driver's side, started the car, and drove off immediately. She told herself not to stare at his hands on the wheel, and especially not to imagine them on her body.

"Don't you have to let it warm up first?"

"It gets warmer if you start driving. You have to ride slow, though, no sudden moves."

"Oh."

They drove past her car in the ditch.

"I see you didn't make it very far. To the restaurant?"

"Yes."

He nodded. "Good. That's breakfast and coffee taken care of too."

"And, no, I didn't get very far," she continued. "I will never get very far in this town. Not like you with your computer science degree and big-data analysis, or Cooper with his start-up."

"Honestly, I'm not as wildly successful as I would like to be," Gabe said.

"That so? Well, I'm a waitress who had to move back in with her parents."

"Some of my favorite people are waitresses."

"Spare me your pity, Gabe."

"You brought it up. I don't see anything wrong with working hard at an underpaid job while doing incredible volunteer work in town. Someone will notice and something much better will come your way."

"That's the plan," she muttered.

"I used to know a woman named Mrs. Dipple who worked at the Hot Spot Coffee Shop. She used to slip me free donuts on Saturdays after I worked at my dad's office as an intern."

"So?"

"So I nominated her for sainthood. She was a devout Catholic and would see the crown of thorns on the toast all the time. Personally I think the toaster needed to be replaced, but that's not the point."

"And the point is?"

"You don't have to have a fancy job title to be a beautiful person."

"I asked you to please spare me," she snapped.

"We're dancing around the real problem, aren't we? Are you going to let me apologize for how Cooper incorrectly reported my speech last night, or keep being grouchy with me?"

"What do you think?" she asked. "I'll keep being grouchy, as you call it, because I haven't had my coffee yet, my car slid into a ditch, and no matter how you paint it, you said some pretty crass, chauvinistic things."

"How about I get you a coffee and apologize profusely?"

"I get coffee for free. That's an official job perk."

He fell silent, navigating the busier roads in town. The world outside the car was enveloped in white fleece. Everything was soft and round, and everyone in it was sucked into its depths and forced to inch forward slowly. Strings of Christmas lights still glowed in a riot of colors in the early morning darkness. As they drove deeper into town, more stores and businesses came to life.

Happy, happy holidays, Lauren thought. What a mess she was making of her own holidays and life. She should have tried harder for a job in the city—any city in the country—and not let her heart drag her back home after college.

Sycamore Cove was a great place to visit as a tourist or to live if you were rich and owned a huge, seaside residence. It could also be good if you worked in tourism, real estate, or as a lawyer. But as a social worker like she wanted to be? Might as well get comfy as a waitress at Les Amis.

At least they had free croissants to go with the coffee. Croissants and coffee helped enormously with frustration. Sexual or otherwise.

Gabe pulled into the restaurant's parking lot.

"Thanks for the ride." She stepped out of the car, but Gabe called her back.

"Yeah?" she asked, stamping her feet. The freezing temperature instantly penetrated her shoes and coat and she shivered. Her throat was scratchy too.

I bet I caught a cold last night. It would serve him right if he caught my germs.

Which made her remember him kissing her. All over. His lips had touched every inch of her skin, especially the places she normally kept lonely and in the dark. That thought sent a flash of heat from her lady bits up through her chest.

"Do you need me to pick you up since you won't have your car?" he asked, bringing her mind back from her flag-waving nether regions.

He was absolutely amazing in the muted lights. Ginger hair and beard—scruffier than the day before—clear, green eyes focused on her, and those damn lips. Those lips that called her name while saying nothing at all.

She didn't feel the cold anymore.

"No," she forced herself to say. "I'll have someone from the committee get me since we have work tonight." She waded through massive drifts of snow to the entrance.

The restaurant opened in ten minutes, and a few

customers waited in their cars. Not even a blizzard could keep the regulars away from Isabelle's croissants and cinnamon buns.

She called hello when she walked in, knocking straight into Greg, who carried a shovel.

"I can't believe you made it," he said, catching her arm to keep her from falling. "I told Isabelle your car would get stuck in a ditch somewhere minutes from your driveway. Can you get the tables ready? We're running late too."

"Sure," Lauren said with a deep sigh. Stuck in a ditch somewhere. That pretty much summed things up.

Isabelle was putting croissants in breadbaskets, and Lauren grabbed one on her way to fetch the silverware and napkins. The buttery, flaky goodness helped her get Gabe out of her head. For another eight minutes, anyway, until they opened.

***

The moment Gabe walked in, Lauren scowled at him, a hand on her hip.

So much for feeling welcome.

"Sit anywhere there's silverware."

He took a booth as far from the few other customers as possible and checked over the menu.

They had regular American breakfasts, but that didn't interest him. He wanted something different from the last time. The smell of fresh bread and croissants was positively enticing. He could date a waitress who worked here until kingdom come.

Lauren slammed a plate and basket on the table and glared at him.

"What'll it be?"

"I'll have *le petit dujuhnay roo-rahl*," he said, stumbling over the French pronunciation.

"*Déjeuner rurale*," she snapped, correcting him. "I want to come out straight with you. I'm pissed at what you said to Cooper. You treated me like I was a good time to be had while you're in town. Jerks talk like that, and just because you're a muscular, attractive jerk—see how I'm being honest here?—you use it to your advantage to get me, and probably lots of other girls in bed with you for wild, unattached sex."

"Lauren," he whispered, raising his eyebrows.

"Shut up. I'm talking. I don't care how wet you make my panties, you are not entitled to get into them or to take them off. So do not try again, understand?"

"Lauren," he said again, hitching his chin at Isabelle, who stood behind her.

"*Bonjour*," the woman said cheerfully. "*Ravi de vous revoir, monsieur! Café?* Such snow outside, I can't believe it. I am happy to see my customers come in, however. *Voilà!*" She poured his coffee, chatting cheerfully, while Lauren fled without another word.

The kitchen door swung shut.

The older waitress continued softly. "Between the two of us, that girl could use some wild sex. She's been so lonely, poor thing. I don't want her to think I am talking to you, though." Then louder, "*Très bien!* Your food will be ready soon!"

Gabe added some milk from the tiny pitcher to his strong coffee. That was some food for thought. What a lovely woman Isabelle was, to worry about her employee's well-being.

He'd have to find a way to make Lauren understand that what guys said to each other wasn't what they thought or felt. It was just talk. Pumping themselves up and getting ready for the fight. The fear of failure was too strong to admit, and he didn't want to fail in Sycamore Cove.

But she had admitted being attracted to him, despite her

anger. A weak spot. His blood pounded faster, as he remembered her words. He'd like to take advantage of the fact he made her panties wet.

Gabe knew how to play games for what he wanted, and sometimes you had to play dirty to win. He wanted to win this game.

He wanted Lauren.

The French waitress brought him a half baguette, boiled egg, sliced ham, assorted jams, butter, another croissant, freshly pressed orange juice, more coffee, and encouragement to get Lauren in bed as soon as possible.

"Such a sweet girl, but really too tense. She needs a man like you to make her feel good," she said and patted his shoulder as she left.

Gabe couldn't agree more. The only problem was getting Lauren to admit she needed him.

Chapter 11

Lauren nodded and rubbed Emma's back as the crying woman downed her fourth tequila in less than fifteen minutes and dissolved into a blubbering, red-eyed, runny-nosed mess on the barstool. Considering that Emma was supposed to be Mrs. Claus for the evening at the Sycamore Cove Boating Extravaganza and raise money for the new animal shelter, things weren't going well for either of them. Not well at all.

Bob, the committee accountant for the fundraiser, stood at a safe distance, shifting from foot to foot. "Should we tell the boating people we have to cancel?" His wife kept him so sheltered, he'd certainly never seen a full-blown breakup crisis starring a twenty-five-year-old in a sexy Mrs. Santa Claus costume in the middle of a makeshift bar.

"No, we aren't canceling." They needed the money they could raise during this boat show. A great number of wealthy people would be here for the preholiday sales and would certainly contribute. That was, if a sexy Mrs. Claus could catch their attention for a few minutes.

They wouldn't cancel. Lauren whipped out her phone like

a weapon. She wasn't the head of this fundraiser for nothing.

Emma clapped a hand over her mouth and stood up, eyes as big as Christmas wreaths. She stumbled for the restroom.

Lauren scrambled to help her stay upright, pocketing the phone.

"I'm so sorry." Emma retched in the urine-stained toilet.

Did Lauren have any disinfectant wipes or gel in her bag? Gross.

"It's okay, we've all been there." Lauren had never experienced the particular humiliation of having a boyfriend dump her at a boating show, then buy a boat for another woman, but hey, she knew heartbreak.

Emma leaned over the porcelain bowl to give it another go.

Lauren held her hair and patted her arm. She was particularly familiar with the kind of heartbreak that drove you to drink too much cheap alcohol and then puke in a filthy, malodorous public restroom.

"Sleep it off tonight. Tomorrow you'll feel like crap, so try and take care of yourself. Burn anything he left at your house. That always helps."

Emma nodded and let Lauren help her outside and to a cab.

Four phone calls and four rejections later, Lauren was ordering a tequila shot for herself. She had called the only four women she knew who fit a size 2–4, were between five foot five and five foot ten.

The answers were painfully clear: no, no, *no*, and maniac laughter before the no.

Shannon had sounded horrified at the idea, and Abby had laughed at her. "I love you so much, I'm almost tempted. Except I have things to do tonight that don't include displaying my tits and ass to old fogies."

"What things?"

"Terrible things with my girlfriend. You don't want to know. Hugs!"

Lauren was out of candidates and ideas. She had asked Emma and Emma's boyfriend to be Mrs. Claus and an elf helper to drum up cash during the show for the shelter, and if she didn't find someone cute, skinny, and dumb enough to put on the costume and beg rich men to donate, she would lose a lot of money.

And she needed every available penny. The cash hadn't exactly rolled in like she had hoped after the bake sale.

The glass of tequila was at her lips when the last person on earth she wanted to see strode between pristine white boats toward the bar.

He was cocky and confident, fitting in with the well-to-do clients at the show in his business jacket and dark slacks, dress shirt unbuttoned at the top. That tiny triangle of chest skin commanded her attention.

She tossed back her drink, puckering her lips at the vile taste. Apparently, her awful day was going to begin and end with Gabe making it worse. In fact, he had made the whole day horrible. Isabelle had dropped the terms *handsome, redhead,* and *libido* at the restaurant like she was seeding a field.

Now Gabe was at the Boating Extravaganza. How had he known? She hadn't told him where she would be this evening.

"Having some problems with your volunteers?" Gabe asked, taking the stool next to her.

"Why are you here?"

"Because you're here." He waved to the bartender. "I'll have the same." He frowned at the drink when it was set in front of him. "Want to tell me about it?"

"No, I don't. How did you find me here?"

"I have my sources...*Mrs. Claus.*" Gabe swallowed his

drink with a grimace. Then he smiled wide.

"Don't say it," Lauren warned, a sinking feeling in her gut. "Don't—"

"I dare you."

She shook her head. "We aren't playing anymore. And besides, it isn't your turn for a dare. It's mine."

"Then dare me to do something so it will be my turn again. You have to admit, this dare is better than the snow."

"You really can't let this go, can you? All right. If you want to play, then I dare you to spend the rest of the holidays with your parents in Boston and let me get on with my life!"

"Not a fair dare. It has to be something I can do here that's not illegal or will cause bodily injury."

"Who says we're playing a fair game of dare?" Wait a minute. She'd just started playing his game again. Dammit, she had to stop doing this to herself.

He stood from his stool and cleared his throat. From that nonexistent distance she could feel his body heat rolling from his chest. "You don't want me playing an unfair game where illegal is on the table, do you?"

She heeded the warning in his voice. She didn't want that. For some reason, it made her picture herself on a table.

"Lauren," Her contact for the boat show called as approached them. He shook her hand. "So where is our Mrs. Claus and her helper? The yacht is ready for them."

"Right here," she said, motioning to herself and Gabe. "We had some delays because of the snow and have to change. We'll be there in five minutes."

***

"We?" Gabe asked when the man left.

"Yes, we. I. Dare. You." Lauren held up a velvety green-and-white bundle of cloth and fluff.

"Another costume?"

She nodded.

"And that's my dare? That's it? Dress up as...what?"

"Mrs. Claus's elf helper."

He could feel the grin coming on. "This shouldn't be a problem, not after the stripper pants from the other night. I dare you to dress up as Mrs. Claus."

"Not a problem? Just wait until you put it on."

Five minutes later, he was ready to accept defeat.

Tights. A skimpy tunic-shirt with an open V nearly to his belly button. Candy canes in his belt. What the hell kind of outfit was this?

Then Lauren came into view through the crack in the bathroom door.

His only problem getting dressed was pulling his tights over his erection and hoping it wouldn't show.

"Ready?" she asked breathily, her front-laced corset squeezing her breasts up to her chin, and skirt flaring over her hips.

"What exactly are we doing? We don't have to pop out of anything and dance, do we?"

"We have to entice people to give us money for pictures with us, and hopefully they'll want us to sit on their laps so badly, they'll give us lots and lots of money. Then all that dough goes to the shelter. Also, the organizers pay us to be Christmassy and cheerful. Do you sing?"

He couldn't take his eyes off the tops of her breasts. If they fell out of that corset, he was a dead man. "'One Hundred Bottles of Beer on the Wall,' sure."

"How about 'Jingle Bells,' 'Deck the Halls,' or 'Good King Wenceslas?'"

She tugged on his belt and tunic, getting the candy canes aligned just right. The view. Oh God, that view was either going to kill him or make him drag her off to a cabin in one of the yachts.

"Good King Who?" he asked.

"Great. I'll lead, you just hum the choruses. Okay, follow me." She pivoted, and for the first time he noticed her legs. Curvy and embraced by thigh-high white stockings that stopped at the skirt's hem. She threw him a green hat and some black, curlicue shoes.

"I'm not wearing these," he said.

"You are if I'm wearing *these*." She held up a pair of patent-leather, stiletto, lace-up boots with fake-fur toppers.

She yanked the boots on, exposing her white-lace undies and creamy thighs. He wasn't sure how he was going to walk out there with the beginnings of his raging hard-on. He forced himself to bend in half and get the ridiculous shoes on and jammed the hat on his head. At least gingers looked good in green. It was small consolation.

He followed her swishing skirt and bright red costume with more faux-fur through the crowd, taking one long step for every two of hers.

"How tall are you, anyway?" he asked.

"Five foot two."

"No, you aren't."

"Close enough."

As they continued through the hall, Gabe kept staring at Lauren. Her costume definitely put him in the holiday spirit. He started smiling until he realized he wasn't the only one noticing how luscious she was.

Heads turned from every direction. Jealousy simmered in his gut and he opened his hands wide to keep from making fists. This dare was his fault. It was his dare and his—

Someone slapped his butt as he walked by. A group of thirty-something-year-old women stood clustered together, laughing and sneaking peeks at him.

His fault.

Okay. That wasn't humiliating. Right. He kept going. The tights were like ants all over his legs, and the shoes, cheap props that they were, plier-pinched his toes. Fucking hell. Women were insane to wear such shitty clothes. Why would anyone do this on purpose?

To raise money for a no-kill animal shelter.

He focused his attention on Lauren's swaying ass and the flashes of pale thigh from under her skirt. It might not have free coffee, but at least this job had perks. He lifted his chest, winked at a young mother checking him out, and gave it his everything. For the fundraiser. For Lauren.

Chapter 12

They reached the finest yacht on display in the huge hall. A few people with Boat Extravaganza badges greeted them and showed them aboard, up the steep ramp. At the far end of the deck, there was a Christmas tree, ornate seat, a pile of presents, and a small table.

"For pictures and donations," a young man explained, pointing. "We'll manage the prize table. People donate, put their name in the bucket, and depending on how much they give, they can choose their prize: a gift, an ornament, a picture with Mrs. Claus, a chance to win the speedboat, or a mix. We'll let you know who gets what."

"I stand by the chair?" Lauren asked. Her cheeks were flaming. "What does Gabe, my elf-man helper, do?"

"He will hand out the gifts or ornaments, and if someone wants him in the picture, he does that too. Mrs. Claus, you actually sit on the armrest here, looking naughty and nice. Oh, that's perfect."

Gabe's pressure spiked at the sight of her perched uncomfortably like someone's toy.

The man clapped his hands. "Okeydokey, I think we're ready!"

People started coming to the table after their tour of the yacht to donate and sign up for a chance to win the prize. After a dozen people went through the line, Gabe came to the conclusion that this had been a massive mistake on his part. His feet hurt, his tights were driving him mad, several women had squeezed his ass like they were testing ripe grapefruit, and if one more kid giggled at his legs, he was going to toss them overboard.

That wasn't what made him really mad, though.

Lauren was smiling. A plastic, mile-wide, teeth-baring grimace as yet another sleazy man beckoned to have her take a seat on his lap.

In as nonthreatening of a manner as he could manage, Gabe strolled closer to help her up after the photographer caught the moment. "How long are we doing this?" he asked under his breath. He wasn't sure how much longer he could keep from bashing heads together.

"Tell me, is this the shittiest job you've ever done, or have you done worse? Personally this ranks right up there with the summer I shoveled horse shit every day during a heat wave. You?"

"I think they call it manure, and this is the worst. How much longer?"

"Don't tell me you regret your dare?" she asked.

He didn't answer.

"About four and half more hours."

"Four and a half—"

She coughed. "Why do you think I didn't volunteer to do this in the first place? Please try to look extra sexy when single women come through so they'll want a picture with you. The shelter gets everything above the three-dollar prize-entry fee."

"What do you mean?"

"The first three dollars go to the boat people. But everything above that goes to us. Sing along with me and try to get everyone's attention."

She broke into a rousing rendition of "Rudolph the Red-Nosed Reindeer."

"People can ask me to be in a picture with them?"

She nodded and kept singing, gasping for air as often as the song allowed. A man with a slicked moustache, wearing cowboy boots and hat, sat in the chair. He patted his lap eagerly for Lauren to sit.

Gabe resisted the urge to kick his curlicue shoes up the man's ass. This was his dare. His fault. The man put his hands on Lauren's hips to hold her in place. They smiled for the camera. He kissed her cheek and slipped a hand under her skirt before releasing her.

Lauren thanked him for his generous donation.

He stared at her tits.

Gabe's vision went red. His fists were pummeling the man's face and everything was bloody. He was pelting customers with presents and insulting every perv who had dared touch Lauren. He was swinging the Christmas tree like a club and—

"Gabe!" Lauren hissed. "Help the nice lady get the tree ornament down!"

He snapped back to reality where he wasn't beating anyone up and plucked the decoration from a high branch.

"Lauren," he whispered, "who did you have lined up for this job originally? The girl who canceled?"

"Her name is Emma. She's a pole dancer, and she asked her boyfriend to lend a hand. But he's a spoiled rich kid who had enough of her and decided to buy a boat for his new girlfriend five minutes after arriving."

"A pole dancer who didn't have any work colleagues who could fill in for her?"

Lauren gaped at him and he could see her face-palming mentally. "I would have had to pay whoever filled in. Emma was doing it as a favor because she loves dogs. Damn. I should have thought of it, though. I could have offered free croissants or something."

They split for several photos, Gabe's blood on a slow boil. Worst fucking dare ever.

A pole dancer.

"How did you know I would be here?" Lauren asked.

"I was talking to Shannon when you called her."

She frowned, and then fake smiled. "You should have stayed with her. I'm sure you'd be having an exciting evening by now."

"You know the schedule for your events is posted on your Facebook page, right? It wasn't hard to find you."

"Aren't you glad you did? I am," she said.

A kid came up behind him and snapped his tights, snickering.

"Hey, watch it!" Gabe snarled, then remembered he had to be nice. "Or you'll get on Santa's naughty list. You wouldn't want that, would—?"

"Santa's a fake shithead and you look stupid. Like a girl!" the little brat said.

His mom shushed him halfheartedly, undressing Gabe with her eyes. "That's not polite, Mikey. Why don't you stand over with Mrs. Claus and tell her what you want for Christmas while Mommy gets her picture taken?"

She waltzed up to Gabe and wrapped an arm around his waist. "Can I tell you what I want for Christmas, or should I just let you surprise me?"

Gabe muffled a groan and gave a smile that would make

his high school drama teacher proud. Any chances he had of getting hired by the very conservative governor of Virginia would be shot to hell if these pictures were tagged.

He had a sudden vision of a bored intern surfing on the web, searching for #sexyelves, and getting an eyeful of his nearly-bare chest and green legs. Or #hotredheadstrippers and seeing the black stripper pants being ripped off him by an eighty-year-old.

The governor would never understand. This was the best opening in Gabe's field of study for a government job he had seen since graduating. The fact that he found it right after being laid off and that the interview had gone so well made it seem like fate.

Lauren wasn't the only one who had goals of making the world a better place one project at a time. If he positioned himself well, he could go far and do great things. He had to get the job.

But this particular governor wouldn't appreciate his staff moonlighting at anything they had to get half-naked for.

The mom got in one more pinch to his ass and blew him a kiss good-bye.

A vein twitched and throbbed in his temple.

Why did this place bother him so much more than the retirement-home ladies getting full-body hugs or the knitting society cheering him on while he stripped?

Meat. That was why. Those elderly women had looked at him as though he was a human being—albeit a sexy and toothsome human. But these people looked at Lauren and him like they were meat at the market. Not to mention the bratty kids.

Muscles knotted until they cramped, pressure built up in his head, and he had to bite back more and more insults. Most of the people were friendly or indifferent, but the lecherous ones more than made up for the rest. Hours passed.

Lauren's hair was disheveled, circles appeared around her eyes, and her forced Christmas spirit was falling flat. No wonder, he thought. She had put in a full day at the restaurant. Yet another man had her on his lap. His hand moved up her corset to rest on the underside of her breast.

Christmas tree. Bashing. Blood.

He shook his vision clear. "That's it. We're done here." He took her hand and pulled her out of the man's hold. Turning back, he hissed, "You even look at her again, and I'll take you outside and beat you to a pulp before you can whimper."

His voice must have sounded convincing. The man shot out of the seat and scrambled to escape from the yacht.

Gabe zeroed in on the Boat Extravaganza worker. "We're done. Thank you, and everyone have a nice evening."

"But we've got another half hour before the show closes," the man whined.

"I'll loan you her costume. You'll look ravishing in it, I'm sure."

He guided Lauren down the ramp and through the crowds as quickly as his damn shoes and her ridiculous boots would allow, barely containing his urge to hit something the whole way.

***

Lauren let Gabe take her with him. Fatigue smothered her like a wet, woolen blanket, and at that point she was willing to follow him anywhere that was off the yacht. He shoved his way straight through the crowd, creating a path.

Nothing mattered but sitting down—and not on a pervert's knees—so she could take off the boots. The boots. Oh God, the boots were killing her slowly from her feet up.

Her toes had gone numb, except now that she was

running, each step sent pins under her nails. The arches ached and her calves begged for mercy. The torment ate its way through her legs and into her back.

Through her sluggish mind, images of her day flashed by. Carrying dishes around, smiling endlessly at people who didn't deserve it, hands all over her rump and waist and hips while Christmas carols and holiday songs skipped merrily along in the background. Christmas was hell.

"If I get out of here without killing someone, it will be a miracle." Gabe led her into a back room and pressed the Lock button. Their clothes and things were stashed on the floor, and a table held a water cooler.

He poured himself a cup, motioning to Lauren he would pour her one too.

She nodded.

"Worst fucking idea ever." His face was mottled red and a vein throbbed in his temple. "How did you come up with that shit for your shelter?"

"What?" she asked, choking on her water. "It was your fucking idea to dare me to be Mrs. Claus. So I'm not allowed to dare you back? Do you think you had it worse in your elf-boy tunic than me in my fluffy, short skirt? And this corset. I haven't been able to take a decent breath for hours."

"Why was this one of your activities? You should have known how it would go. Those men feeling you up, like you're some kind of a...a..."

"A what? Some kind of pole dancer? I had a *professional* lined up for this job! You dared me to do it! It's your fault I spent my evening in these heels after working all day, getting my ass rubbed against old men's crotches. I hate you."

"I hate you right back! I'm never going to get hired at this rate. I might as well call Emma and get some fucking lessons. Why am I even here?"

"I don't know. I dared you to go home to Boston and leave me alone." She pressed a hand to her heart, the top half of her chest heaving for air.

He reached for her in alarm. "Are you all right?"

"I can't breathe in this damn thing." Stars flashed and died in her eyes. She tore at the laces on the front of her outfit but couldn't get the knot undone.

"Here." He pushed her fingers aside and started to work at the knot. With each swell of her chest, he grazed her breasts. The haze of exhaustion lifted as nerves tingled.

"Dammit," she muttered and grabbed his nape to pull him in for a kiss. She couldn't get enough of his lips no matter how hard she pressed on them. Only her need for air was stronger. She tipped her head back, taking shallow gasps.

He wrapped his arms around her waist to lift her onto the table. Wedging his legs between hers, he leaned in, lips against her ear. "You could have warned me. I thought I was going to have to kill someone out there." He yanked on the laces. The tie came undone, freeing her from the corset.

"Tonight was your fault." She was overheated and tried to catch her breath after hours of too little oxygen. What was he doing to her? Blurring the lines of her emotions. She needed him and wanted to slap him. "You're driving me crazy."

"I'm not even trying yet." He pulled the corset open and bent down to kiss her breasts. She leaned back on the table, bracing herself with one arm, the other on his shoulder.

"Wrap your legs around me. I want to feel if your panties are getting wet."

"You'd like that." But she lifted her legs. His lips traced moist trails along her chest, and her nipples peaked. She wanted his lips on them. Her panties were definitely wet.

"I've wanted you since I saw you for the first time at the hotel." He cupped her breasts from the costume and brought them together to suck at both nipples. She would have fallen backward on the table, but he supported her. "God, you're hot. I can feel it through these damn tights."

She squeezed her legs so the bulge in his tights pressed against her aching, needy sex. He was going to bust through his pants, his erection strained against the fabric so much.

"Take off my panties."

"And do what to you?"

"Take them off, Gabe, I need you to...to..." She couldn't breathe with his hand grazing up the bare skin under her skirt, tickling and teasing.

He tugged one edge of her panties and she brought her legs together so he could pull them over her boots.

"Do this to you?" He pressed gently on her knees to part her legs.

"Yes, and more."

He knelt in front of her, a wicked half smile making him devilish. He licked up the middle of her sex.

She gasped and the beginnings of an orgasm tingled upward. So fast?

"No fingers, my hands aren't clean."

"Do it again, please. What you just did...."

He descended again between her legs, and she fell back on the table to let him do whatever he wanted to her.

Heat and wet pressure consumed her. She closed her eyes and lost herself in the feeling. The word *relentless* came to her. He'd said that word. Relentless in his pursuit of taking her to places she'd never been. Her orgasm started rippling, then it shook her to the core and she bit her hand to keep from moaning aloud or yelling his name.

She'd never come so hard or so fast in her life. Crazy, he drove her absolutely crazy. He began to stand and back away.

"God, Gabe, don't stop." Without a care for her dignity,

she was ready to go on her knees and beg him to take her. She wanted to feel his hard cock up to the hilt inside her. She wanted to feel him come.

"Later," he said hoarsely. "I don't want a quickie with you. I want you on a bed, calling my name while I take my time with you."

"I can't wait for later. I need you inside me now." He didn't move. "Now, Gabe. I want you now."

He slung her bag, which held his clothes, onto the table and found his wallet. In a heartbeat he had pulled down his tights, opened the condom, and rolled it over his wide erection. Then he took his time to maneuver between her thighs.

"You want me to fuck you hard right here on this table?" Lifting her legs, he pressed his cock to her entrance. He paused, staring down at her, waiting for her approval.

"Now." She used her heels to dig into his buttocks. He slid in with exquisite pleasure.

"All right, but afterward, I'm taking you home and doing this right."

He backed out, showing his control was stronger than hers and then thrust in quick. She gasped and rocked with him. He moved faster, each thrust filling her and shaking her. Holding her hips to keep her in sync, he rammed her to the core until there was nothing left but him and his movement.

Every nerve tingled and hummed from the top of her head to her feet, and she begged him to keep going, to keep her in this needy place, but she also wanted him to take her somewhere. Pleasure climbed. He moved inside her, and all she could do was hold on as she lost complete control of her body. She was his at that moment, whatever he decided to do to her, and her climax crashed into her like a train. He shook her apart until she was pieces on the table and held her as the rocking slowed and she was whole again.

He breathed heavily into her hair, his arms clasped around her. Her focus came back and she remembered where they were.

She had to hope no one had heard them over the brouhaha from the show floor. They were still half in and half out of their costumes.

"I've never screwed an elf in green tights before," she said, catching her breath.

"I've never screwed a married woman in patent-leather boots before." He seemed inordinately pleased with his accomplishment. His conceited grin broke through her pleasure-induced, lethargic state.

Wait. Wait one fucking second. She had just screwed Gabe. Why did she do that?

Besides barely knowing him, she was mad at him, no matter how mind-blowing the orgasms.

Two orgasms in ten minutes. That was a record.

Maybe there was something to be said about having sex with men who drive you crazy. Nerves tingling and good cheer racing though her body made her reconsider her position on no sex with Gabe simply because he talked trash to her brother. It was sort of a moot point by now, anyway.

"I suggest we try to find a hotel room." Gabe pulled their clothes from the bag and stripped, yanking the elf tights off with a vengeance.

She had to swallow at the sight of him completely exposed. His nonchalant stand and command of his tight, muscular body made the drab back room disappear.

Turning her attention to getting her Mrs. Claus dress off, she didn't realize he had stopped dressing until she felt his hands on her bare shoulders. She was standing, and despite her heels, he had to bend low to kiss the curve where her neck met her collarbones. Closing her eyes, she basked in his delicate kisses.

More of this at a hotel? Yes, please. Oh yes, *please*! She moaned as his kisses turned to nibbles.

But her feet screamed bloody murder and sooner or later someone was going to try to come in there. "Let me change and we'll go."

Chapter 13

Lauren followed Gabe as they hurried through the boating show and out to his car. He peeled out of the underground garage, flipping the heater up to max.

"Tell me if it's not warm enough," he said. One hand strayed to her knee.

"It's not warm enough," she said, teeth chattering. She really needed a new coat. This unusual cold snap would be the death of her.

"Give it a minute, but if necessary I'll make an emergency stop for skin-to-skin reheating."

She snorted, smacking his shoulder. But not so hard they would swerve off the road and crash.

"No, truthfully, I have no idea where we are going, but I would really rather get you naked when we get wherever we are headed."

"Take the next left," she said and guided him to one of the only hotels in town. As soon as they arrived at the six-floor building, they ran laughing into the reception area.

They were still grinning at each other until the clerk

announced they were booked solid until Sunday. Christmas Eve. Today was Friday.

"Booked solid? How is that possible?" Gabe asked, waving his hand in a question. The counter pen flew in the air. "How many people vacation here?"

"Between the boat show, the tree-decorating contest, and relatives who don't want to sleep at their in-laws', quite a few," the woman replied in a slow drawl. She replaced the pen. "I know I wouldn't stay with my mother-in-law if she had a bunker during the zombie apocalypse."

"Right," he said. "Any other places we could try?"

"There are a couple of dives out past Highway 75, if you don't mind creepy-crawlies. Otherwise, the Portside Hotel is the only other clean one in town. They are more expensive, so you might get lucky," she said in a tone that predicted they wouldn't.

"Come on," Lauren said, hooking her arm in his. "Let's go over there. Give it a try."

As they walked to the car, a frosty gust picked up, biting through her coat and stinging her face. Temperatures that evening were right at freezing, and it was supposed to snow some more. Another thought chilled her more than the wind, though.

He was with Shannon today.

"All right, Gabe, time to be honest. You told me you were with Shannon when I called her this afternoon to ask if she could be Mrs. Claus."

"We were standing together, yes."

"So do you have something going on with her?"

"Will you believe my answer?" he asked.

"Depends on what you say."

"She called me because they found an article of clothing in the side room we were in for the cake. Asked if it was mine, and said if I was in town she could meet me and let me see it. That was it. You happened to call right as she was handing me a glove that did indeed belong to me."

"I see. Can I trust you while you're here in town? You won't play games with others behind my back?"

Gabe stared, confusion wrinkling his forehead. "Just like that, you're asking if I'll be faithful for the next three days?"

"Yes. Am I your only fun for now?"

"Lauren, I swear you are the only woman I have right now. Here, in Boston, elsewhere. The only one."

Something in his voice sent little shivery snowflakes dancing through her stomach. She shouldn't get nervous or excited about being his only squeeze for a handful of days. It wasn't as if that was any particular achievement.

"Okay. Tell me if it changes before you make a move on someone else. That's all I ask." She played her *I'm too mature to jump on you in public card* and kept walking.

"Hey." Gabe stopped. He tilted her chin toward him. "You have got to be the coolest girl I know."

"No doubt. I drink beer and shoot pool too."

"Oh my God. I have to bend you over a sofa as soon as possible."

"Who says I'll let you bend me over a sofa?" She tried to sound offended, but the idea was already warming her up.

"Do you want me to bend over the sofa instead? Interesting. Or I could sit on it and you could sit in my lap."

She smacked him playfully again.

"First you need to direct me to a pharmacy and then to the Portside Hotel."

"A pharmacy? Oh. Yes. Of course." He needed to buy something important. "Take a right out of here and straight on to Oakway Avenue."

After a few turns, they reached the historical downtown,

found a spot to park in, and walked a couple of blocks. The old-fashioned streetlamps and bright Christmas lights on all the buildings kept the darkness and gloom at bay. The snowy ground and ice sparkled, and despite the cold, Lauren was warm with happiness.

She was strolling arm in arm with the most amazingly sexy man she ever met. So what if this was only for a couple of days? It was like an early Christmas present wrapped up in a ginger bow. The holidays weren't so awful after all.

They found a pharmacy so Gabe could choose a box of condoms—it didn't escape her notice that he bought two. He had goals, that was for sure. She helped herself to the bowl of peppermints by the cash register.

She popped the candy in her mouth as they left the store. The crunching snow under their feet accompanied them as they walked across the town square, holding hands. Decorated Christmas trees were all around them.

Gabe suddenly tugged her hand to pull her into the large, wooden gazebo in the middle of the stone paths and park benches.

"When I was young, I always thought this would be a great way to impress girls," he said.

"What? Running around in a park with two boxes of condoms?"

"No. Look up."

In the archway above her head hung a bushy bundle of dark green leaves and white berries.

"To kiss under the mistletoe," he said, lifting her chin. He didn't kiss her right away, though. He simply stared. And he kept staring.

"Gabe?" she asked. "Are you going to kiss me?"

***

Gabe didn't know what to say. What he didn't tell her was that when he was a kid, he'd thought kissing under the mistletoe was romantic. In his prepubescent mind, he had imagined he would kiss his wife that way. Years and relationships had jaded him since then.

And yet he had always avoided the Christmas custom until now. Without stopping to think, he had acted on his heart's impulse to drag Lauren over here. But their agreement expired in two days. No complications, no emotions, that was the deal.

He wanted to kiss her so badly he ached.

This was all wrong.

And terrifyingly right too.

Closing his eyes to the winter night and Lauren's lovely face, he bent forward. His lips found hers and brushed them softly. The cold skin of her nose tickled his cheek. She leaned into him, parting her lips and sighing. The world disappeared until she was his world. He held her tightly, deepening his kiss. His tongue darted in and tasted the peppermint she had picked up. His favorite Christmas candy would never be the same without her lips.

"Lauren! I thought that was you," a woman cried in his ear.

Lauren broke free of his embrace. Then she screamed. The shaggiest dog he'd ever seen barked and jumped in excitement. Lauren screamed again and dodged behind him while a woman dressed in hot pinks and yellows scolded her dog and told him in vain to sit.

"Ralphie, you know Lauren doesn't like it when you bark. Quiet! Quiet!" She yanked his collar, dragging him down the gazebo steps and into the snow, where she tied him to a post.

Lauren stopped trying to crawl onto Gabe's back and simply held on to him as though she feared for her life. He wasn't quite sure how to react.

"Should we get out of here?" he asked, twisting his head around.

"No. I'll be all right. I just need a minute." She was panting and her voice came out small and breathy. "I'm...I'm afraid of dogs."

"You're afraid of—?"

The vision of Lauren holding the brown-and-white stray puppy as if it was a huge tarantula flashed before his eyes. He had seen she was afraid of dogs at the bake sale but hadn't believed it.

"I don't think we've met," the woman said, cutting through his thoughts. She stomped into the gazebo, shaking loose snow and dog fur from her coat and hat. Her hand was outstretched to shake his. "I'm Josephine Hall, but you can call me Aunt Jo if you're a good friend of Lauren's."

He shook her hand reflexively. "Pleased to meet you." He remembered vaguely Cooper talking about his crazy, cat-lady aunt who lived in town. "I'm...a good friend of Lauren's."

Damn. Cooper was going to find out about them, whether he announced his real name or not. It was just a question of when.

"Oh, that's so nice. I love meeting Lauren's special friends. Do you know Cooper, her brother? Such a sweet boy. Always running around. And Lauren, my busy bee. She's going to save the animals from that old torture-chamber animal shelter they have now, did you know that?"

"Yes, I did." Lauren still hadn't surfaced from behind him, and he could feel her trembling. Ralphie barked and she jerked. He reached around with both arms to try to comfort her. "It was lovely meeting you, but I'm afraid we need to leave. We were just out shopping."

"It's nearly ten in the evening. You kids these days and your schedules. Lauren," she said, circling around to find her niece, "let me give you two a little something. I just so happen to have some extra cake with me left over from my Bible study group. Where is it?" Aunt Jo produced the biggest carpetbag he'd ever seen and pulled out a lunch box. It thumped in a strange way. Was her cake made out of bricks?

This seemed to revive Lauren, luckily. "That's sweet of you, Aunt Jo, but we have to go. You'll have some cake for us at Christmas, right?" She had recovered from her fear now that the dog was firmly attached, and edged toward the stairs.

"I have another cake that's been aging for four months. Here, sit down real quick. You can have it before you go. That way you don't buy any fast food to snack on. You wouldn't believe the unnatural additives they put in that stuff. Terrible."

Before he could protest, Aunt Jo forced them to sit on a bench, then put napkins and small pieces of hard, brown cake in their laps. Aunt Jo took a big bite, smiling at them. Lauren nibbled at hers and glanced pointedly from Gabe to his cake.

What was this about?

The dog barked, straining at his leash and jumping again, and Aunt Jo turned to reprimand him.

"I dare you to swallow," Lauren whispered in Gabe's ear. His gut clenched up from his balls to his throat when her lips brushed his skin.

"What?" Over half her cake had mysteriously vanished.

"I dare you to swallow it," she said, canting her chin at his portion.

"You dare me?" He chuckled. "You do know I'll dare you right back?"

"Mm-hmmm. And I'll count myself the luckier of us both, because I know if you dare me to swallow, it won't be this cake." She licked her upper lip, exaggerating the movement to make her purpose clear.

He wanted those lips on him. Now. "One bite?"

"Yeah. If you can do that, you'll go down in the annals of Sycamore Cove, but you have to swallow all of it. Especially if you want me to swallow all of whatever you give me."

The thought her swallowing all of something in return—and he knew exactly what he'd pick—was too hot. He shoved a huge bite of the strange-smelling cake in his mouth. He immediately realized the problem. A brick mixed with sawdust and a handful of spices would be easier to chew.

The overpowering cinnamon rose to his nose, making his eyes water. Pieces of old fruit stuck to his teeth, and the dry, hard mass of cake refused to be moistened as he mashed it.

He was going to lose this dare.

"Do you like it?" Aunt Jo asked.

He blinked watering eyes and bobbed his head in a half nod.

"I use a bit of rum to cook it, but then moisten it for ten weeks with a mixture of molasses and sugar water. Alcohol tends to ruin everything it touches, don't you agree?"

He nodded, jaw grinding away.

"Finished mine already, Aunt Jo!" Lauren announced cheerfully.

"You want some more, sweetheart? There's plenty."

"You know I have to watch my figure during the holidays, but thanks." She patted Gabe's knee. "You are now experiencing a true Sycamore Cove Christmas tradition. Aunt Jo's cake is…famous in these parts."

"Mm-hmmm," he managed. He started to swallow a bit. It stuck. He coughed.

"I always say coffee is what this cake needs to bring out the flavors," Lauren said. "We'll pick up a cup on the way home. Which, by the way, I'm getting cold, sitting out here."

He forced it down his throat, choking. The smoky, tarlike aftertaste of too much molasses clung to his tongue. He wished he could scrub out his mouth with a brush dipped in vodka. Or he could drink some straight from the bottle.

"We'll see you in a couple of days," Lauren said and gave Aunt Jo a hug. "Can you get Ralphie?"

"Oh, of course, sweetheart! I'll never understand how anyone could be afraid of such an adorable mutt, but that's life. Don't worry about Christmas, I'll have him and the cats rounded up and locked away in the basement. Will your friend be coming too?" Aunt Jo asked, going down the steps to untie her dog.

"I think he's going home to his parents' house. And speaking of family, can we keep my friend a secret between us? Don't mention him to Cooper or my parents until I can talk to them, please."

"Oh, of course not. I remember what Cooper did to the last boy he thought you were dating. Such a shame about his nose. Well, ta-ta!"

Aunt Jo waved a mittened hand in farewell and dragged a frolicking Ralphie out of the snow-filled square. Lauren fidgeted nervously until the dog was gone. The wind had entirely died off and big, fluffy flakes slowly descended. As soon as they left the shelter of the gazebo, her hat and shoulders were lightly powdered.

She was too charming. He pulled her into a hug so he could nibble on the tiny bit of earlobe exposed by her knitted hat. He could feel her trembling through their coats.

"Are you all right?"

"Yeah, I'm used to it. You can keep doing that to my ear."

He sucked gently on the lobe.

"Mmm, yes. Just like that."

He had to stop before he lost control and started stripping. He kept doing that around her. "You know that dare bordered on harmful, right? Someone could get killed trying to eat her cake."

"I'm sorry, the temptation was too strong." She didn't sound too sorry.

"I told you I was too hot to resist. Now to get you to the hotel, and don't think I won't make you sweat with my dare."

Chapter 14

Getting herself in trouble on purpose felt strangely freeing. For the first time in Lauren's life, she didn't worry about their status together or what would happen tomorrow. In past relationships, sex had been a serious, calculated step taken after discussions and waiting to make sure everyone felt comfortable, which at the time had seemed the right thing to do.

But she was ready for fun, and Gabe's roaming gaze and promises sent shivers of anticipation through to her most secret nether regions. A quickie at the boat show was only the beginning, and she couldn't wait for the rest.

She would go on her knees again if he wanted. She would swallow whatever he asked—she wanted to drive him wild.

Her pace quickened when she pictured him in a steaming bath, skin slick and glowing in candlelight. She would drag her teeth across his shoulder while reaching down into the water. Then the real world slid out from under her feet. For a split second, she hovered before falling hard. Right on her ass.

Gabe spun. "Lauren, are you all right?"

"I slipped." Pressing her hand on the sore spot, she started to climb to her feet.

Gabe scooped her up in his arms. "Your derriere is going to require a lot of ice and attention," he said, carrying her the rest of the short way to the car. "A bucket's worth of ice."

***

Gabe set her in the passenger seat and she winced. *Please don't let it be serious.* A broken tailbone would take months to heal. He could forget making her pay for daring him to eat that awful cake. That would be a travesty.

"How bad is it?" he asked as he climbed in the driver's side. More importantly than worrying he wouldn't be able to do the thing he wanted to do to her, though, he hoped she wasn't in pain. "Do you need to see a doctor?"

"Luckily I hit the left cheek mostly. It feels tender but not too bad."

"Then a couple of applications of ice will suffice. You still want to go to the hotel?"

She gave him a knowing grin, one eyebrow arched. "Afraid you won't get a chance to dare me? I'm ready to go."

That was the fastest he'd ever driven on icy streets. At the hotel, he escorted Lauren through the front door into the bright lobby. Relief washed over him at the sight of a male clerk standing duty at the counter. He hadn't exactly told Lauren the whole truth about his encounter with Shannon in town, but it wasn't going to be an issue.

"Hey, can I let you get started?" she asked. "Save half the bill for me, but I'd like to take a quick look at my backside in the bathroom."

"No problem," he said. "But I'm not letting you pay half the bill." Damn his savings. He wouldn't take her money, especially not for a hotel room.

She limped off to the bathrooms and Gabe continued to the counter. At the same moment the clerk asked how he could help him, Shannon stepped out of the office.

She drew up short, her scowl melting away.

"I can take care of Mr. Nicholson," she said, motioning the clerk to move. He nodded and trotted off, leaving Shannon staring hungrily at Gabe.

Not good. He racked his brain for a precedent on how to handle this situation, but nothing was coming up. How could he book a room without her thinking he was there for her?

He'd try to play it cool.

"Shannon, hi. This is a bit last minute, but I need to know if you have any rooms available for tonight."

"For you? We should still have something. Let me see." Her nails clicked on the keyboard and she glanced up at him several times. "As I mentioned when I gave you your glove, we do have a room. Should I go ahead and put you down for one night? Two? More?"

She leaned forward to give him a better view of her breasts, pushing her elbows into her ribs. Now her nails were clicking on the counter in a slow beat that made him break out in a sweat. "I hope you stay for a few nights, at least. The hotel has so much to offer in the way of a pleasurable time. I'd be happy to discuss things further. In private."

He cleared his throat. Playing it cool wasn't working. It was time to tell her the facts.

"One night for now, and the room is for *two* people," he said.

"I thought it would be," she said, then licked her lips. "I'll put a star by the checkout date so you can extend it for as long as you like. I have no doubt your stay will be satisfying—"

The bathroom door at the side of the lobby opened, and the clack of boot heels reverberated across the floor.

Gabe didn't have to look to know it was Lauren—Shannon's expression said it clearly. She stiffened, lips twisting back into a scowl. Her fingers flew over the keyboard, tapping like a rainstorm.

Lauren's perfume wafted over Gabe and her hand slipped into his.

"Hi, Shannon. Were you able to find a room for us?" Lauren asked in a friendly voice. There was no gloating or snark, but Gabe was afraid it wouldn't matter.

"As I was just telling Mr. Nicholson, we have one suite available. Unfortunately, all the standard guest rooms are taken." She gave them a fake smile. "It has an ocean view, of course. It will be $540 a night, plus taxes. Should I go ahead and book?"

"Yes," Gabe said, not allowing himself to consider refusing.

"No," Lauren said. "That's too steep. I'm sure there are other...hotels."

"The motels outside of town might still have some rooms," Shannon said. "I would take cortisone cream for the bed bug bites, though. Thanks for stopping by."

"Shannon, please reserve the suite," Gabe said.

"Gabe," Lauren said under her breath. She turned sideways to continue. "It's too much for one night. I have no intention of letting you pay for it all, and I can't cover half."

"And I have no intention of letting you pay for any of it," he replied quietly. Shannon huffed, probably rolling her eyes, but he wasn't paying attention to her.

He had just enough money in savings for a couple of months if he was careful. If he got the job in Richmond, he wouldn't have to worry about anything. If he didn't and nothing else popped up, he would be in deep shit.

But this was worth it. He wasn't taking Lauren to a cheap,

dirty motel outside of town. Thriftiness be damned.

"We'll take the room," he told Shannon.

She nodded, mouth clamped shut. In silent rage, she prepared the paperwork, had them sign, and slapped the card key on the counter. She left before explaining where the room was, stalking off to the office without so much as a "have a nice evening."

Lauren picked up the cards. "I don't think she took that very well."

Gabe put his arm around her shoulders, leading her to the elevators. Shannon was already far from his mind. "How did your ass look?"

"It was round with two cheeks, and a red spot where I fell."

"You'll probably have a terrible bruise. We'd better hurry and get that ice."

They got lost once trying to find the suite in spite of the signs. Lauren finally had a hunch that an unmarked staircase had to go somewhere. Bingo. The second they stepped inside the suite, they stopped acting civilized.

In a frenzy of kisses, grasping hands, and nipping, Gabe backed her to the bed and helped her sit. She had her legs parted slightly and yanked on the top of his jeans playfully, and he was rather disappointed when they didn't tear off like the stripper pants.

"So tell me. What do I have to swallow?"

He shook his head. "First I need to check that left cheek for a bruise and to apply some ice. Then I'll have to get rid of the taste of the Christmas cake. After that, we can talk dares. Let's get those clothes off you."

He stood back to watch.

She stared at him, eyebrows pinching together. "What? You want to watch me undress?"

"Does that seem weird to you? Because I think it sounds like a great time," Gabe said. "I'll help get you started if you want to give me a foot."

He pulled one leg up, and holding carefully on to her calf, slipped her leather boot over her heel and off, taking advantage of the situation by skimming the ticklish underside of her foot.

She jumped, surprised. Then she handed him her other leg. "Do this one too."

Strangely enough, she didn't appear to be used to men taking care of her. Well, that was about to change, and he almost felt sorry for any future boyfriends. If he let her have future boyfriends.

Don't go there. This is a holiday special that ends in a couple of days.

She sighed in pleasure as he took off her second boot and lightly rubbed her heel, arch, and toes through her wool sock.

"Your toes are a little wet. Your boots aren't suited for the snow."

She fell back on the bed while he massaged her foot, and she lifted her head to answer.

"I know. I spent my extra money this month on my fundraiser. Don't worry, I won't melt," she said. "That's not true. I'm kind of melting right now, and if you keep doing that, I'll die and go to heaven."

He gave an extra rub just to hear her moan. Then he set her leg down and stood over her. "Time's up, Lauren. Take off your clothes."

"With the light on?"

The room was very brightly lit, and the off-white walls of the large suite were practically glaring.

He flicked off the main light switch, leaving two reading lamps on at the head of the bed. "How about that?"

"Why am I the only one undressing?"

"My question exactly when you put me in a cake and watched from the back of the ballroom. Did you think I wouldn't notice you and your friend? Just be glad I'm the jealous sort and want to keep you all to myself, instead of inviting a bunch of people to watch. Clothes off. Now."

She slid to the middle of the bed, her gaze riveted to him. When she reached the center, she came up to her knees, pulled her large sweater up and off, and began to unbutton her slacks. She had a loose, silky camisole on like she'd worn the other night that hid her breasts and bra from his sight.

Too damn slow. He crawled onto the bed with her and took matters into his own hands. The slacks went to her knees, and he wrapped his arms around her waist. "Face the wall and go on all fours for me."

She was breathing heavily and he kissed her jaw to her ear and then down her neck. He cupped one breast through her clothes so he could kiss the top of it as well. Her nipple hardened through her bra and his cock jerked in agony in his jeans despite his recent release. He needed her again, and soon.

"Turn," he said and maneuvered her to face the wall. She went on her hands, leaving her soft, round ass in his hands. He finished taking off her pants. "Tell me if this hurts," he said. Sliding the panties over her rump and smooth thighs, he touched the left cheek, looking for marks or bruising. She gasped softly. A few red splotches marred her skin, but he was careful to avoid them. "Are you all right?"

"Yes," she said over her shoulder. "Are you going to just stare at me all night?"

The view was amazing. Her pale, winter skin was golden in the faint light, and her curves enticed him closer. No, he wasn't going to stare all night. Not with the need to take her coiling in his core, tearing his patience to shreds. Sweat prickled on his forehead.

But he wanted to drag out the time. He had promised her.

He moved in to brush her bare skin with his jeans, teasing her. He could see she was growing moist, and he bent in for a taste.

She slapped the mattress, scraping her nails on the blanket the second his tongue touched the folds and entrance of her sex.

"Oh, Gabe. You're going to have to get a condom soon."

"No, I'm not." He backed off the bed. "I have to get some ice first. Don't go anywhere."

"Whoa, what—?"

He left her protesting as he went into the hall to find the ice bin and to fill a small bucket. When he came back, she had stripped off the rest of her clothes and was entirely naked in the middle of the bed. He nearly lost his will to apply the ice.

"Your medical needs come first," he said, pretending not to notice her desirable body on display. He couldn't just jump on her like a Neanderthal no matter how badly he wanted to. This time, she had to beg him to fuck her before he would take any pleasure for himself, and even then he might make her wait. The night was going to be long. "Ready for your ice?"

She crooked a finger at him. "That's not what I want, and you know it."

"Oh, but that's what you're getting. Hold still."

She drew back as he stalked her like his prey, ice wrapped in a face towel. "Not afraid, are you?"

"Maybe."

"Do you need any painkillers?"

She shook her head. "I don't think I need that ice, either. An orgasm would do me a world of good, though."

"Shouldn't neglect an injury. You went down pretty fast.

Ideally, the injured area should be elevated. Like this." He rolled her sideways to have her on all fours again.

She narrowed her eyes at him but did as he wanted. Then he very lightly pushed on her shoulders to press her chest into the bed, leaving only her beautiful and bare derriere in the air. He had to admit he was rather pleased with the result.

Nothing left to do but take full advantage of the situation.

"Gabe, I'm not sure about this position," she said. "It's kind of humiliating."

He ran a finger up the back of her thigh.

She gasped.

"This," he placed a quick kiss on the outside of the same thigh, "is elevating your injury to reduce swelling."

"Whose swelling?"

"Yours, of course." He placed another kiss on the inside of her thigh, right next to her sex.

"Really?" Sarcasm dripped from the word.

"Yes. Tell me if you're uncomfortable in any way. Are you ready?" Without waiting for her answer, he gently pressed the ice pack to the dark marks where she had fallen.

She hissed. "Damn that's cold! What is it with you and— ?"

He cut her off by using his tongue on her tender folds of her sex, reveling in her warm, wet readiness. Despite their quick romp in the backroom at the boat show, she was hot and needy, and he worked her thoroughly with his mouth. Every shiver that went through her shook him as well, and he kissed and explored her body, experiencing her pleasure as his.

When she made little whimpering noises and called his name, he paused to rub her clit using the pad of his thumb.

"Gabe, I need you now." She twisted the bedsheets in her hands and writhed, but he held her and the ice in place.

"Stay like you are." She surprised him by obeying. He

loved to see her exposed like this, bowing down and waiting for his touch. "Do you want me to take you like this? Or is it humiliating for you?"

"Like this. I just need you now," she said through clenched teeth. "But take the damn ice off ass!"

He tossed it to the floor. Still fully dressed, he continued to stroke her clit and sex until she moaned. He inserted two fingers inside her and felt the fluttering of an oncoming orgasm.

"Finish for me." The words came out rougher than he intended, but he was losing it. "I want to hear you call my name."

"Gabe," she gasped, squirming beneath him. He kissed up the length of her spine, never stopping his exploration of her sex. She said his name louder when his mouth reached her nape.

He breathed in her delicate scent—a mix of perfume, shampoo, and sweetness that belonged to her. He nibbled on the back of her neck, taking in her every movement and sound. She let him lead and he took her higher, moving his other hand under her breasts pressed firmly to the bed. He stroked a puckered nipple, squeezing it softly.

She rubbed her face back and forth against the sheet, panting hard. "Yes, keep going."

He bit back a groan. Only if he could keep it together.

He pulled at her nipple and she moaned her approval. He slipped a third finger into her sex and rolled her nipple firmly. The walls of her sex convulsed and she arched.

When she called out his name and shuddered with an orgasm so strong she started to collapse, he nearly came in his pants like some high schooler.

"Ready for more?" he asked, holding her to his chest.

She reached up to stroke his bearded cheek. "Am I ever."

"Turn over, I want to see you."

He unzipped his pants, freeing his erection and rolled on a condom slowly. Drinking in the sight of her, waiting and naked before him, he took his time. It was necessary. He had to calm down before he could touch her.

"I don't get to see you?" She started to undo a shirt button, pouting.

"Not yet. I want you focused only on yourself. This is still all for you."

He crouched before her on his knees and guided her legs over his thighs. From there, he reached up to cup her face and leaned in to kiss her lips, eyelids, and cheeks lightly. He was intensely aware of his erection stroking the outer folds of her sex. Desire burned through his veins, consuming him.

"I said I was ready," she said, grabbing his hair in both fists.

Not yet. She had to beg. Cupping her full breasts, he sucked hard on first one nipple and then the next, nipping with his teeth when she scratched down his back.

She was so hot against his cock. He knew she was even hotter inside. The tip of his erection was at her entrance. She hooked her feet behind his back, moving under his t-shirt to get to his skin. Tightening her hold, she tried to draw him inside, much as she had at the boat show, but he held her hips away and continued to tease her breasts and neck.

She gyrated softly against him, showing she was ready. "Gabe," she begged. "Please."

"Look at me."

She fixed her eyes on his, the golden-brown irises a thin ring around her black pupils.

"You are so beautiful."

Pinning her to the bed, he leaned forward, sliding ever so slowly into her depths.

Her nails dug into his arms.

***

Lauren was going crazy with need. He gave her exquisite torture when she wanted him to take her fast and wild. She sucked in her breath and strained to meet him, biting her lip as the sensation of him filling her took over her body. The base of his cock reached her clit, and he twisted to press on it, heightening both their pleasure.

He slid out of her again and a whimper escaped her throat.

"Harder," she pleaded.

Gabe pulled out, leaving her empty, and she bucked upward to meet him. His cock pushed at her entrance, spreading her wide, and he angled his hips to thrust.

But again he taunted her with aching slowness, a sweet glide to her center. A tingle of pure pleasure lit up in her core, piercing straight to her heart. She gasped for breath.

"Look at me," he commanded. At some point she had closed her eyes. He was staring down at her, his green eyes dark with desire. She was his. She gave herself to him for this moment.

Another delectably slow movement and she took his wide erection into her, rolling her hips to bring him in farther. Her sex began to clamp down on him, and she was trembling. A hot rush of new wetness flowed outward.

"Gabe, please, oh, please." She writhed with urgency, with a need she didn't know she could feel.

His body responded. Pulling out and driving back in hard, he moved faster.

She grasped his buttocks, diving into his pants so she could feel the muscles tightening with each thrust.

"Hold on," he said.

She arched backward, bucking her hips to meet him and

exposing her breasts. He took one nipple in his mouth and sucked hard, and she fisted his hair in answer. He thrust again, banging the bed into the wall, and she had a moment of regret for the neighbors. But it was a fleeting thought as she lost control. All she could do was gasp for air and urge him on faster with her hands and hips. She shuddered and dissolved into pieces beneath him as her orgasm hit, flaming up and outward through her body.

His own release followed, his every muscle popping with the strain, and his cock throbbing inside her. For many heartbeats, he simply held on to her, and she didn't want him to ever let her go.

Then she realized they had slid to the edge of the bed. Her head was hanging off.

"Is this what you meant by elevating my bruise?" Lauren asked, laughing and righting herself. "Because I can't stay like this for long."

"Then we'll have to reapply the ice." Gabe made a grab for the melting ice and threatened her with it.

"Don't you dare." The second the words came out, she knew it was the wrong thing to say.

He tackled her to rub an ice cube down her front while she laughed and tried to fend him off. She finally grabbed him for a kiss—a deep, time-stopping, heart-aching kiss in a tangle of lips and tongues, hands and arms, legs and bodies twining together.

A kiss she didn't want to end.

He must have been feeling something similar. "This is too good to stop at Christmas," he said, tucking a strand of hair behind her ear.

"What do you mean?"

"I mean, why should we stop getting together when I go home for Christmas? You can come visit me. Or I'll visit you."

"What?" What did that mean? This was supposed to be a short-lived, casual-sex thing. Was he interested in more between them? Or just more sex? "I didn't think—I mean a long-distance…are you suggesting an arrangement?"

Chapter 15

"Would that be so awful?" Gabe asked. Lauren appeared horrified at the thought of a long-distance entanglement. He didn't see what was wrong with a friends-with-benefits arrangement, but she didn't seem interested in continuing anything with him past Christmas. "Don't answer that. I'm just saying we don't have to pretend this never happened. We could still see each other after I go home."

As he said it, he remembered that if the job in Richmond came through, he would only be an hour away by car. That would be something. Longing raced through him. Spending cold winter nights with Lauren in his bed was more than a job perk. It was winning the fucking lottery. His breath caught in his chest, and he held it, waiting for her reply.

"Secretly?" she asked. "Behind Cooper's back and without telling anyone? Just for sex?"

When would she make a decision without worrying about her brother's reactions? He shrugged in resignation. "If you don't want him to know, then I won't tell Cooper. But don't think I'm ashamed or afraid to tell the whole world, and it isn't just sex. It's mind-blowing sex."

What the hell was he saying? This was getting into dating territory. He didn't want to mess with this sort of complication.

She grabbed him for another kiss, and his misgivings vanished. "But don't tell anyone yet," she said, blinking at him with her irresistibly huge, brown eyes. Damn, she was good at that. "It would ruin Christmas. You have to understand, Cooper wouldn't take it well."

"I'm getting the idea. Are you hungry? Let's order room service."

She sat back, sighing. "I hate to sound pathetic and penniless, but here's the truth. This month, I am pathetic and penniless. I know I still live with my parents and should have at least some cash, but I was hit with student loans, car repairs, a trip to the dentist, and Christmas gifts, not to mention several administrative costs for the fundraiser, all of which is to say, I can maybe afford some toast. Get something for you, but I'm fine."

Penniless and pathetic? He wasn't about to tell her the truth about his own situation. "Lauren, let me be your sugar daddy and buy you dinner." He had enough to splurge on food. Besides, he quite liked the idea of taking care of her in more ways than one.

"I'm a modern girl. I don't need your money."

"But you want my hot body, right? You'll have to keep your strength up, trust me on this one. What would you like?"

***

After a steak-and-potatoes dinner, red wine, and another round of wild sex while bending over the back of the aptly named love seat in the middle of the room, Lauren slept better the rest of the night than she had in months. Since she didn't have any pajamas, she took Gabe's t-shirt, leaving him to sleep nude. Which was perfect for snuggling.

The morning arrived, intruding on her wonderful rest by letting a piercing beam of light into the room. It shone straight in her eyes, pricking like needles through her lids until she knew she wouldn't be able to sleep anymore.

A wonderfully sexy man was holding her. Gabe. Gabe Nicholson had his arm around her. She curled in closer, her whole body pressed to his.

He was too sexy to leave alone. She pulled herself up, straddling his narrow waist and kissed his shoulders, neck, and bearded jaw. His cock jumped to life, hitting her rump, and she began to grind on him.

"Good morning," she singsonged.

He breathed in deeply, eyes opening. He grinned up at her.

"You can say that again." He guided her movements.

"Did you forget to dare me last night?" she asked, remembering she was supposed to swallow something. "Why don't you do it now?"

"Because I have other plans for you."

"But you could dare me to swallow anything you want."

"If you are referring to my morning erection, I'll have you know I don't dare women to swallow. They beg me to let them swallow."

"What?" she asked, sitting up straight.

He flipped her over effortlessly and found a condom on the nightstand. He tore it open with his teeth.

"You heard me. I'll wait until you beg." As soon as he had the condom on, he spread her legs with his hands and entered her slowly, watching her expression.

She kept her face angry. For about three seconds. God, she couldn't resist this man. She needed every inch of him inside her, and pretending she didn't love it was impossible.

How many orgasms had she had in the last twelve hours or so? Way too many. She was probably in danger of having a heart attack.

He did that trick of rubbing her clit with his thumb that made her forget her own name, and she rolled her hips to meet his movements. If he wanted to use her body and make her beg for more, fine. It wasn't clear if she began to buck her hips faster or he was riding her harder, but before she knew what hit her, an orgasm was shaking up through her core and setting off fireworks from her toes to the top of her head.

He continued to thrust throughout it, a conceited grin on his face. Then his orgasm slammed him and he pulled her into his arms. His release pounded through his erection and she clung to him while he lost himself to it.

"Hey," she said. He didn't let her go but kept her close to him. He smelled wonderfully warm and masculine. She burrowed her nose in the slope of his chest. "Still with me?"

"I can't uncross my eyes," he said.

She laughed while checking his face. He was fine. "Are you busy today?"

"Yes. I'm booked all day banging the walls here with you."

"No, you're not."

"Yes, I am."

"Yes, I mean, no." She sat back, pulling the sheet over her legs so he would focus on her face. "I have to do some work, but if you're already busy you can't go with me."

"I'm going wherever you are going today," he said.

"Wait before you make any promises. What would you say if I dared you to crash a ritzy party the mayor is hosting this evening so I can have a chance to talk to him about the animal shelter?"

"Crash a party? That the mayor is having?"

She nodded, using her wide-eyes trick to try to disarm him.

That usually worked like a charm.

"I'd say you shouldn't waste your dare."

"Oh. I understand." She glanced away. "It's no big deal. I'm sneaking in with Abby as a florist, so she'll be with me. You don't have to go to keep me company."

"No, you don't understand." He wrapped his legs around her. "You don't have to dare me to crash a party with you. I would be honored to be your uninvited date tonight."

She launched herself at his hot body for a kiss.

After that, they had to get busy. Gabe drove her to Abby's apartment so she could get cleaned up and borrow a slinky dress.

Lauren had sent several letters to the mayor's office, asking for support for a new animal shelter. He wrote back, but always in a wishy-washy, noncommittal tone. Trying to see him in person at his office had also been a bust. The man was too busy and had canceled the one time she managed to get an appointment. Basically, Mayor Thompson agreed they needed to move on this project, but he didn't necessarily have it in the budget. However, if she could raise enough money and community support, perhaps he could find the rest of the funds in the budget. Of course, she was doing her best, but many people wouldn't give money for a new building that might not even be built.

She was going round and round in frustrating circles, trying to get the ball rolling in the right direction.

Sigh.

Double sigh.

Tonight, she would try to give Mayor Thompson an updated file of photographs, testimonials, amount of collected donations and promises of support, including the gift of land by the retirement home. If that didn't sway him to find the rest of the money needed, she didn't know what would. The outdated shelter was a place of torture. No other words sufficed to describe it, and the town could afford to do much better.

After Gabe drove into Abby's parking lot, Lauren reminded him to borrow a business suit from Cooper's wardrobe, gave him a quick kiss good-bye, and ran up the stairs to her friend's apartment.

Abby threw open the door before she could knock.

"I saw you guys drive up!" She started to squeal and jump up and down.

Lauren motioned her inside. "I can't tell you the details, because I don't kiss and tell, but, oh yes." For the yes she dropped her voice an octave, like a soft moan in memory of the orgasms Gabe had given her.

Abby did a happy dance, pounding her feet on the floor. "We must drink to this."

"Not yet. I need to shower and get cleaned up. I'm grungy from my night of love. Then we can toast," Lauren said. "What time do we meet your mom?"

"At three. Plenty of time."

Which meant she had less than three hours to get ready, not exactly "plenty" of time. Lauren rushed off to the bathroom, borrowed her friend's shower gel and shampoo, asked for a spare toothbrush, and styled her hair as best as possible without her usual array of products. It would do. She was mostly a natural girl, anyway.

Abby, being tall and whip thin, was not the same size as Lauren but did have a collection of clothes left over from past girlfriends in a drawer. Among this pile, Lauren scrounged jeans and a sweater for work and a sparkly gold cocktail dress that had a fitted bodice and tulle skirt.

"Please tell me you have shoes that go with this," Lauren said, holding it up.

"That fit you? I doubt it. There's a sale on at Your Inner Sole. We'll swing by on the way to my mom's."

New shoes would be torture if she had to stand a long time, but it was her own fault for not being organized and getting an outfit together weeks ago. Her depressingly empty bank account hadn't helped, either.

"Great. Let me call Gabe and give him a heads up. We can stop by Isabelle's, too, for some croissants. I'm starving," Lauren said.

They grabbed their coats and bags holding their changes of clothes and stepped out into the cold winter day. The air rushed over her, and Lauren bent her head against it.

Tonight was her Hail Mary pass.

Putting up jars for pennies in local stores wouldn't help anymore. She had to take it to the next level or the shelter would never see the light of day. And she was tired of knowing these animals were suffering. Her Aunt Jo reminded her every time they saw each other, not that she needed reminding. Her nightmares were enough.

The silent jaws clamping on her arm, phantom pain lancing through skin, muscle, and bone. Yellow teeth and dead eyes.

She took a trembling breathe. The car door screeched as she opened it too fast and climbed inside. No, she couldn't stand aside and see people or animals suffering. Not when she could make a difference.

If the mayor didn't see things her way, though, she couldn't do much about it besides smother her sorrows in croissants and chocolate.

She was ravenous by the time they reached the French restaurant and talked Isabelle out of a basket of her baked goods.

"You know I love you, right?" Abby told her, stuffing her

face and driving toward the shoe store.

"I know." Lauren took a huge bite of the flaky, buttery yumminess. "Eat some chocolate at the same time as the croissant. Trust me."

Abby did as she was told, groaning loudly as the chocolate melted and mixed with the croissant on her tongue. "Damn, this is so good. Will you marry me?"

"Not yet. Gabe wants to be my sugar daddy and feed me fancy food so we can have lots of sex."

Abby nodded. "I can respect your decision in that case."

They reached the shoe store and flew through the selection. The shimmering, gold stilettos Lauren found promised to be horribly uncomfortable, but they were half-off and would look gorgeous. Next stop, Abby's mother's flower store and not a minute to lose.

Lauren sent a text to Gabe to have him meet them at the restaurant where the mayor was hosting his party. He replied, sending a winking smiley. Was that supposed to mean he would be there? Not be there? Coming but already drunk?

The seaside mansion had been converted into a breathtaking restaurant with a huge wrap-around porch, gabled windows, double doors with stained glass, white rocking chairs, and a gazebo nearly as large as the one in town, all overlooking the beach and water.

Gabe was leaning against his rental car when they pulled into the long drive, Abby driving her car with Lauren behind her mother's work van. He sauntered up to the van to open the sliding-door for the flowers. Several staff members greeted them and showed them the ballroom to be decorated. The three of them began carrying in the ornate flower arrangements Abby's mom had prepared.

Getting in was easy.

This party was an annual tradition for the mayor, so the

staff had their parts down pat. Gabe and Lauren took orders and tried to make themselves useful as assistant decorators, but neither had any idea what to do. Whenever he was close enough, Gabe stole quick kisses.

"Did you find something nice in my brother's closet?" Lauren asked when they were alone.

"No. He asked about you, though. He was wondering what happened to you last night."

"I'll send him a text saying I'm with Abby. So you don't have any evening wear?" How would they blend in if he had his jeans and boots on? Not that he looked bad. His ass looked particularly nice in the fitted jeans.

"Stop checking me out, you'll make me blush." He winked. "Don't worry. I have a solution in my backpack. You realize someone will recognize us, don't you?"

"That's why I gave you the hat to wear and I have my hair in a ponytail. We're like Superman. No one will ever recognize us after we change."

He didn't argue with that logic. Actually, if they had fifteen minutes of mingling time before getting kicked out, it would be a Christmas miracle. But it would be enough if she moved fast.

"All right. Where should I put this big thing?" he asked.

Lauren pointed to an empty corner, but a staff member redirected him. They would have to be subtle about sneaking into the bathrooms, and they could only come out once there was a good crowd. Maybe this was a bad idea. Getting arrested would be the death warrant of her new shelter. Plus, Gabe had to be a model citizen to get the job with the Governor.

The last decorations were in place, and she adjusted and readjusted the same ribbon to hide her shaking hands. This wouldn't work. They had to go.

Gabe took the ribbon and plumped it for her. "It's about

attitude."

"What is?"

"Having fun when and where you shouldn't. We're going to hide now." He glanced both ways. All of the staff and hired help were busy elsewhere.

"I don't think—"

He grabbed Lauren and Abby and herded them to a hallway at the other end of the ballroom. Then he motioned for the girls to follow him down the narrow way.

They hurried to the restrooms. Gabe gave her a nod right before the ladies' room door closed and he was gone.

They were going to pull this off.

She and Abby each locked themselves in a stall and changed clothes as quietly as possible. Hopefully, no staff would need to use the facilities and no guests would be in this part of the building and notice anything out of the ordinary.

Lauren shimmied into the sparkly dress. Really shimmied. This thing was designed for someone with much less boobage. Like a cup or two less. At least the skirt wasn't too short.

"You good?" Abby asked.

"Yeah, and you?" Lauren slipped on her heels and found her jewelry. She let her hair down, shaking it loose so it would fall in its natural curls, then applied her makeup.

They waited more or less patiently for another fifteen minutes until the sounds of arriving guests told them it was safe.

Lauren sent Gabe a text. *Ready?*

Ready.

Chapter 16

Lauren couldn't believe her eyes. And here she had thought Gabe was red-hot in jeans and boots. Where had he found a tux?

"You look outstanding." She wanted to whistle, but it would make too much noise. They hid their bags in a dark corner and began to stroll down the hallway.

He coughed, extending his arm for her to take. "Thank you. You look...very nice as well. You remind me of Mrs. Claus. I met her a couple of days ago, but I must admit, you are classier than her."

Abby snorted. "I'm going on ahead since you two are ignoring me anyway. Maybe I'll get lucky and the mayor's daughter is a lesbian. I've heard she's a total babe." She hurried off, Lauren and Gabe arm in arm.

Lauren's stomach fluttered, her nerves gnawing at her courage with each step she took. This was a mistake.

"I can't." Lauren gulped for air.

"You can," Gabe said. "We need to talk to the mayor. We are concerned citizens, not here to cause any trouble. You can talk to him."

She shook her head. "I can't. I've never done, I never do, this isn't a good idea." If she went out there, she would throw up on her new shoes. Or worse, she would throw up on the mayor's shoes in front of all of Sycamore Cove's finest society.

***

Of course it wasn't a good idea. It was stupid. That was obvious from the second she asked Gabe to go. But she'd done that thing with her eyes and she had been half-naked. Refusing had been out of the question.

So the mayor might throw them off the property. Neither of them would go to jail. Besides, it wasn't as if the governor would be there and decide not to hire him.

Lauren had her hand on her chest, and her face was ghastly pale.

Time for a pep talk. First rule: never admit the plan is stupid. If he had stopped once to think about how stupid it was to put on stripper pants, sell hugs while draped with tinsel and a kitten, and then crash a mayor's party in the same state where he was trying to get a job with the very conservative governor, he would have gone home to Boston long ago.

Too late now.

Pushing on a door that said *Staff Only*, he pulled her into a small janitor's closet.

"All right," he said. It was a tight fit for the both of them and it smelled of lemon-scented cleaners and old rags, but it was the best he could offer.

He turned on the light and shut the door. "Listen to me. It is a good idea. This is for a worthy cause. This isn't about you or me getting free shrimp or caviar on crackers or champagne. This is about your fundraiser and the animals it will help." He paused to see if this had any effect and instantly regretted it.

She chewed a finger, her eyes shiny with tears, but that wasn't all. Her breasts. Dear God, her beautiful breasts were falling out of the top of her dress. And he couldn't take advantage of the situation.

"Maybe," she said. "But if security gets ahold of us and we get arrested, the mayor will never follow through with the project."

"We'd have to be truly obnoxious to get arrested. The worst they'll do is escort us off the premises and say threatening things like, 'The next time you show up uninvited, we'll call the police!'"

"You're sure?"

Her breasts. Don't look at her breasts. "I'm sure. I've done this before. The second we go out there, head for the buffet and get a glass of champagne. You'll look like you belong and it will steel your nerves. Right?"

"Right. Okay. Let's go," she said.

"Um, Lauren, I have to let you go without me for a couple of minutes."

"Why?"

He shifted uncomfortably. "You could say I need to calm down before going out in public."

"Calm down, as in...oh." She glanced at the tented bulge his erection made in his pants. "You do need to calm down. It's too bad I can't help you with your big problem. If only you had a dare you wanted to use. But you wouldn't use a dare for a sexual favor."

"I'm not that desperate." He was almost that desperate, especially after she licked her lips and "accidently" brushed against him while moving toward the door.

"Too bad. Because I don't beg." She leaned in to kiss his cheek chastely, and her hand cupped his straining erection and balls. He was dying. "I hope I see you out there soon."

She reached for the door. He stopped her, coughing. "And if I did dare you to do something that wasn't exactly illegal, certainly not harmful, but probably morally reprehensible considering we're in a janitor's closet, what would you say?"

"I'd be shocked." She squeezed his balls. "I was told you are so hot and desirable that any normal woman would beg you to take your cock in her mouth."

That did it. "Lauren, I dare you to put my cock in your mouth."

She gasped in mock surprise. "And do what with it?"

"And swallow when I come." He took her by the nape and drew her close to nibble on her earlobe. She shivered in his arms and rubbed his erection harder. "I. Dare. You."

Her hand snaked into his pants and found his erection. He growled softly, inarticulate as a flash of pleasure streaked fire through his gut.

"Double dare me," she said.

"I double dare you."

"Triple dare me." She teased the sensitive skin along his shaft.

"I triple dare you." He had to clamp his mouth closed when she wrapped her hand around him and squeezed.

"Double-dog dare me?"

"Woman, I'll do or say anything you want," he said. "Please."

"Why, that almost sounds like begging. Put your jacket on the floor for my knees." Her sultry command sent his heart beating faster and his erection pushing against his pants even harder than before.

He folded his jacket and put in on the floor for her while she tugged his belt loose. She undid the button and watched his face as she unzipped the opening and finally freed his cock from its confines.

"Like this?" She licked the tip, catching the drop that had pearled there and sending a shock through his body. Then, she delicately placed her lips around his cock and sucked.

He hit the wall behind him so as to not fall on the floor. "Yes, like that." He took her hand in his to show her how to slide and up and down the shaft. She began to suck and rub her tongue in concert with the back-and-forth movements. From deep in his balls, a tidal wave of pleasure built, growing with every second. He fisted her hair, careful not to impede her mouth's movements.

"Yes, Lauren, keep going just like that." A mindless urge took over his body. His hips thrust, and he couldn't stop if he wanted to. And he didn't want to stop.

She picked up speed, and the warm wetness of her mouth, along with the pressure on his erection, was incredible. Part of him wished it would continue forever, but the rest of him clamored for release. She sucked harder and his orgasm crashed through him. He held her head in place as she prolonged his pleasure, lips clamped tight on his cock. The tidal wave that had been building hit hard, and all he could do was hold on as it submerged him. Muscles convulsed and his lungs gasped raggedly for air.

He fought to remain standing.

Lauren had a terribly self-satisfied smirk on her face. She rose, dusting off her skirt and knees. "I swallowed."

"Yeah," he said, voice rough. "I noticed."

"So that means the next dare is mine?"

He nodded weakly and attempted to get his pants and jacket back on correctly. That had been, hands down, the most brain-cell-killing blowjob he had ever experienced. He would never feel the same when smelling lemon-scented cleaners or old rags.

"Ready?" she asked, still grinning at him.

"I might need a moment."

"You're fine." She took his arm, then opened the door slowly and checked the hallway. "I think this calls for a glass of champagne."

***

Walking into the large room filled with flowers and well-dressed guests felt strange after what Lauren had just done to Gabe in a closet. She wanted to giggle and laugh. If these rich, society people only knew what she and Gabe had been up to.

Then her stomach twisted and she checked the corners for a good place to be sick. She stayed on Gabe's heels as he headed for the champagne on the large buffet table; he took a glass for her first and clinked his to hers in a toast.

"To success and a new animal shelter."

"Success," she echoed.

Over a dozen guests filled the room so far, most in dark tuxedos or elaborate evening gowns similar to those Gabe and Laure wore. At least they blended in. It was only a question of time, however, before someone recognized them either as the florists or as a waitress at one of the most popular restaurants in town. Which meant Lauren didn't have time to waste.

She gulped the champagne. The fizzy, sweet liquid warmed her insides instantly, and she took the rolled-up file from her handbag. Spotting Abby across the room chatting with a young woman, she squared her shoulders and breathed deeply.

I can do this. It needs to be done.

"Abby has a second copy of the file in case she manages to talk to the mayor, but you don't, so stay close to me. If you get a chance to talk to him, I'll come over. Got it?"

"Mm-hmmm." He managed to look casually cool while chewing crackers and caviar. How did he do that? No one would peg him as a party crasher.

The noise grew louder as more guests poured into the room, talking and smiling. She didn't see the mayor, however. Tapping fingertips on the table while walking past the shrimp, dip, olives, fancy cheeses and fruit, she surveyed the crowd for him—a wiry, energetic black man whom everybody loved. He would be in the thick of things, so he shouldn't be too difficult to spot the second he arrived.

"Lauren?" a man asked at her side.

She jumped and spun.

"Mr....uh, Mr. Carter! What a lovely s-surprise...to s-see you here." Except she shouldn't be surprised he was here. The fact was, the businessman belonged to this scene like a beer bong belonged in a frat house. He was rich, recently divorced and devastatingly handsome in a silver-fox, gentleman style that was bit too mature for Lauren's taste, but she could appreciate his appeal. He was a frequent customer at Les Amis, so she spoke with him on a regular basis. That is, when Isabelle was too busy to help at his table. The French woman appreciated his appeal more than she did, despite being married.

And did she mention rich? Yeah. Like *incredible jewelry, huge yacht, and inaccessible mansion near the ocean* rich. He handed her another glass of champagne.

"It is indeed a surprise to run into you here. I didn't realize you were friends with the mayor," he said.

"Oh, you know me. I'm friends with everyone," she said, going for flippant. Nice try. He wasn't buying it. He put his hand on the small of her back to guide her along the table and farther from the other guests. She had to think fast. "Listen, the next time you come to the restaurant, call ahead and I'll set aside an extra cinnamon bun for you." Isabelle's buns sold like nobody's business, and anyone showing up later than eight o'clock was out of luck.

"Is this bribery so I don't call security?"

"I just need to talk to the mayor for a second about the animal shelter I'm raising money for. I'll set aside two buns."

"You do know this kind of bribery will get you anything you desire?" he asked, a playful glint in his eyes. "I'm joking. You don't have to bribe me with food. I know all about your fundraiser. I've even contributed to it. I might even give more."

"Really?" She wanted to ask how much, but anonymous donations were just that—anonymous.

"So shocked I can be generous? I'm obviously full of surprises tonight," he said.

His hand was still on her back. Awfully odd he was being this touchy-feely. Suddenly Gabe was standing next them, all traces of food and drink gone from his hands. He seemed sharper and taller than usual.

"Hi," he said without any trace of friendliness. "Gabriel Nicholson."

"Oh," she said. Introductions were necessary, of course. "This is Mr. Carter. He owns Carter and Sons, the fine watches-and-jewelry company. Mr. Carter, my friend, Gabe."

"Call me Ethan." They shook hands in a cold, manly fashion.

Lauren didn't know what to say to cut through the frosty air around them.

"Are you here to speak with the mayor as well?" Ethan asked. "Your face looks familiar. Are you on the fundraising committee?"

"No, I'm visiting for the holidays," Gabe said, nodding toward Lauren. He stepped closer to her, as though to push Ethan a step back.

"But I'm sure I've seen you. Where was it?" He narrowed his eyes at Gabe over his glass. "Of course! You were the cake dancer for the knitting society party and the hugs man at the bake sale. I saw the pictures posted on Facebook." He snapped his fingers and addressed Lauren. "You see? I know all about your fundraiser. I've been keeping my eye on it."

That wasn't a gut-wrenching moment at all. Nope.

"Really?" was all she could say.

Gabe drew in a deep breath and his muscles tightened perceptibly in his jaw and neck.

"Yes, well, I've been helping Lauren out as a special favor for the cause. There's not much I wouldn't do to save kittens," he said sharply.

Lauren was at a loss. *Change the subject.* "Have you seen the mayor yet, Mr. Carter? It's really vital I talk to him as soon as possible."

"He should be here soon. Why don't you come talk to a few of my friends and colleagues while you wait? These are people who could make your dream project become a reality."

"Of course." Without a second of hesitation, she crossed the room with the older man to a knot of his friends. If she could get donations, the evening wouldn't be a total loss.

She ignored the pit that had opened in her stomach at the mention of pictures. Whoever had posted the photos of Gabe, she'd have him or her take them down.

Smiles and voices welcomed them, and Mr. Carter made a round of introductions. The tension in her back eased off as they started asking her questions about her degree in social work, how she'd helped the homeless last year, and what she needed financially for the shelter.

Soon, she was opening her file to show them the graphs of funds and statistics on comparable cities and their animal welfare. They shook their heads at the pictures of the current conditions the animals were living in, which wasn't much of a life, and Lauren could practically see the dollars flying into the fund's account.

Mr. Carter gave her another glass of champagne and tipped his head to hers. "It helps to have the right friends, doesn't it? You'll have to tell me why you are working as a waitress when you obviously have so many marketable skills in project management. Perhaps over a glass of wine at my home one of these evenings?"

"Waitressing? Oh, that's...how life is," she said, vision swimming from too much champagne. Wait, was he flirting with her? Did he just ask her to come to his fancy-schmancy mansion and have wine? "Not sure I'll be able to. I'm terribly busy these days."

A hand took her elbow. "Excuse me, ma'am. Could you step outside a moment with me?" a man asked.

She jumped, cringing.

Security! They found her. Shit on a sugar cookie. "Me? What for?"

"We need you to step outside. This way, please."

Her heart sank into her new shoes. One of the staff must have ratted on her. The mayor was still nowhere in sight and she was being escorted out.

Chapter 17

Gabe scoffed as Lauren waltzed off, stars and sparkles in her eyes at the chance to talk to flabby, rich men. The conversation had punched him in the stomach.

Photos of his stripper act had been posted online.

He loosened his tie, sucking in air. Damn it all to the flaming shit pits of hell. He was screwed. And Lauren couldn't care less. His chances of landing the analytics manager job—the job that should be his—were fading by the second. His dream position was fucking going up in smoke. The governor or someone on his staff would find the pictures.

He had told her no photos, and now this. Her project was going to ruin his career.

Plus, she was so caught up in her fundraiser world, she didn't see she was being hit on with a golden sledgehammer. Fuck.

Maybe it was his own fault for playing games. But that didn't change the fact he was the one who would be broke and jobless from now on.

Across the room, the men were all ogling her, staring at

her chest and mentally undressing her like a bunch of lecherous trolls. Lauren pointed at her file excitedly as she explained something and smiled at them.

He grabbed a glass of champagne and told himself he wasn't furious. He should have known better than to get in that cake, and as for Lauren, she was genuinely trying to raise money. It was plain to see from the way she was standing and talking.

That shithead had his hand on her back again. The room darkened and he reached for the gingerbread house to throw.

"Excuse me, son, could I get some of those Parma ham rolls?" a man next to him asked. He was in an old suit instead of a tux and the light glinted off his brown, bald head, but he radiated enough energy and self-confidence to turn a second-rate football team into Super Bowl champions.

"Sure, I'm sorry." Gabe stepped back to let the man get his rolls.

Lauren laughed. The silver-bell sound of it reached him at the table.

He drank his champagne, determined to get drunk.

"Mayor Thompson! Good to see you," another man said, clapping the bald man on the shoulder. "I haven't seen you in ages. How's it going?"

The *mayor*. This was Gabe's chance to walk away and leave Lauren to do her own work. He picked up another drink while the men chatted over the platters of food.

"Fine, fine! I'm just stealing a bite to eat while the pickings are good," the mayor said.

"I understand, absolutely! Listen, don't let me keep you now, but let's talk later, all right?"

The mayor nodded, "Of course, of course!" He turned back to the buffet for more ham and filled his plate.

"You should try the Gruyère cheese. It's the best I've ever

had," Gabe recommended.

"Is that so?" the mayor asked, taking a few slices. "I do love cheese."

"Doesn't everybody? Great party you've got going this evening, Mr. Mayor. The food is wonderful."

The mayor squinted up at him. "It is a nice party, isn't it? And here I thought I only invited people I know this year."

Busted.

"I'm a friend of a friend. A friend's cousin," Gabe said.

"Mmm-hmmm. Tell me something I haven't heard before."

Fuck it. He couldn't walk away. "Actually, I'm here with a beautiful person who has been working her ass off trying to raise funds for a new animal shelter to replace the subpar one the town has now." He went straight to the point. The mayor didn't seem the type who wanted his time wasted. Although, this argument would work better if the person in question wasn't downing champagne like it was going out of fashion on the other side of the room.

"You mean Miss Hall? She's sent me several letters already. I have it on my list of things to work on."

He needed to give him the file. Where was Abby? Craning his neck, he spied her at the far side of the room.

"Did you try the shrimp and sauce yet? They make quite a pair." As the mayor looked for the shrimp, Gabe waved at Abby.

She noticed and smiled, pointing at the attractive woman she was standing with.

Gabe beckoned her with more gusto. Damn these girls. Then he noticed the security going straight for Lauren. Time was up.

Abby must have taken the hint or recognized the mayor because an instant later she was shoving her file in Gabe's hands and giving him the thumbs-up. She disappeared out a side door.

"Mr. Mayor, I understand you can't be rushed into decisions, but I would ask you to look through these documents. Every day spent in these cages is a day of hell for these animals." Gabe flipped through the file to find the dog kennel pictures. He held them out for the mayor to see. "Allow me to remind you, it's not really Lauren or her committee who are waiting on your answer."

Whoever had taken the pictures really knew their stuff. Each picture captured the hearts and souls of these animals from the puppies huddled in a grungy corner and the corgi pressing its nose to the kennel bars, to the cats who had to step over one another in their miniature playroom to get to the scratching post. Only a glacier wouldn't melt when faced with these photos.

The mayor paused, a shrimp held in midair. "If it's not in the budget, it's not in the budget."

"Based on the funds Lauren has helped raise, maybe it should be put in the budget." Gabe flipped to her charts, not even sure if he had the finance page. "People in this community want it to happen."

Security was escorting Lauren from the room, but Sir Rich followed, protesting.

Time to go, go, go.

"Mr. Mayor, I would like to leave this with you for your perusal. I sincerely hope to hear good news about it very soon."

The mayor stopped him before he could escape. "Do I know you? I've seen your picture somewhere."

Gabe's stomach took the second sucker punch of the evening. He grimaced a smile. The picture had probably been of him in a red man-thong and cake icing. With his luck, the mayor was also best friends with the governor.

"You were giving hugs at the retirement home," the mayor continued. "I saw it on the news. You impress me, young man, if you are willing to walk the walk for what you believe in."

"Give all the credit to Lauren, sir." Tension flowed out of his shoulders. "She's the one walking. Not that I don't love animals, of course, but she's the driving force behind this project. I hope you have a nice evening." Gabe set his champagne down and strode to where Lauren and the rich asshole were arguing with the security guard.

"Excuse me, everyone, but we were just on our way out," he said, giving Lauren a pointed look.

She shook her head furtively. "But I was invited..."

"Something's come up, darling. Your brother sent me a message. His house just burst into flames and your aunt has insisted on feeding him her Christmas cake to ease his worries. Right?"

"What?" she asked.

"What?" the rich jerk asked.

"Listen, folks, I need to see some ID to know if you are guests or not," the guard insisted.

"We have to go," Gabe said.

"I'm sure my brother's fine, but I haven't talked to everyone I *need* to talk to."

"Now, people." The guard put his hand on his nightstick.

"Wait one second, I have explained that this young lady is here with me," Mr. Carter said, getting angry.

"No, actually she's here with me and we're leaving," Gabe said. He addressed Lauren. "Trust me. Let's go." He held out a hand.

She bit her lip, and just as Mr. Carter was about to interrupt, she took his hand, nodding.

"Thank you so much for introducing me to your friends.

I'll see you all at the restaurant soon."

Gabe grinned at the old bastard on his way out. He was going home with the hottie, and the troll couldn't do a thing about it.

They ran down the hallway to grab their hidden bags and out the back door in their dress clothes. Abby was already in her car, rubbing her hands to warm them, and she waved, bouncing around in her seat.

"Did you see that? Did you see what Gabe did?" she said when Lauren opened the door.

"No, I was busy. Not a single pledge, though, from those tightwads, and I didn't see the mayor."

"Doesn't matter, cause guess who did?" Abby pointed.

"Who?" Lauren whipped around to Gabe. "You? You talked to him? What did he say?"

"He said he would think about it, but in my opinion the pictures got to him. I bet you money he puts this on the agenda first thing," Gabe said.

Lauren threw her arms around his neck, laughing with joy. "Oh my gosh, I think I might love you."

A hush followed this statement.

"I have to go," Abby said. "I just remembered I have bread or something in the oven." She reached for the handle on the passenger door. "Unless you need a ride, Lauren, I'll see you later?"

Lauren didn't say anything.

"I'll take her. It's no problem," Gabe said. He wanted her in his car.

It would give them a chance to talk about a few things.

***

Love? Lauren, you're an idiot. You dropped the L-bomb!
Lauren followed him to his car, wanting to get out of the

bitter wind as quickly as possible.

"Did you really talk to the mayor?" she asked, partly to redirect his attention.

"I really did. He was nice. He likes Gruyère cheese and Parma ham. I gave him Abby's docs since you were busy chatting it up with the Sycamore Cove Gentlemen Assholes' Golf Club."

"Which is supposed to mean what exactly?"

"Which is supposed to mean you were busy with a bunch of jerks while I was talking up your project to the mayor."

She shifted in her seat to face him squarely. Freezing cold and still rather tipsy, she tried to determine what he was mad about—the fact that she had been talking to other men or that he had spoken to the mayor alone.

"Gabe, I really, really appreciate you speaking to the mayor for me. That was awesome."

"It would have been better if you had done it. He didn't sound too optimistic." He maneuvered the car out of the tight parking lot and onto the road. "Instead of wasting time with your client."

"My client? Because he comes to the restaurant sometimes? Or is this some veiled insinuation that I prostitute myself for money for my project?" Now she was pissed. Was he upset because she had presented her project to a group of men who had the potential to entirely fund the shelter instead of begging the mayor? Who, apparently, didn't want to help her anyway?

"You said it, not me."

"That's right, I said it." Her voice rose. She was yelling. "Yes. I was trying to get money from those men. I have been trying to get money from everyone I see for the last several months, and just because you and I have a thing going on, that's supposed to change? Or I should be ashamed of it?"

"Didn't you see how they were looking at you? They won't give you money. Or if they do it's because your tits were hanging out of your dress."

"Pull the car over."

"No, it's freezing. I need to keep driving to warm it up."

"Pull over now."

He pulled to the curb and stopped but left the engine running.

She grabbed her bag from the backseat and got out.

"Don't," Gabe said. "It's too cold. I'm sorry. I shouldn't have said that. Come on, I'll drive you to the hotel. We can talk there."

"Listen carefully, Gabriel Nicholson. If you ever mention my tits again, I'll make sure my brother hears of it. I don't care what your deal is, but you don't own me. You don't judge me, no matter what my tits are doing."

"Lauren, I'm sorry. I was mad because I could see what they were thinking. That dress, it's..."

"The only dress in Abby's wardrobe that fit me. You think I bought it? Damn it, Gabe, I needed to look good tonight, and this is the only thing I had to borrow. But that doesn't give you the right to say I sell myself. Screw you." She slammed the door. She was in the middle of nowhere and it was freezing cold.

After buttoning her coat and pulling on a pair of pants over her shoes and under her skirt, she began to trudge through the snow on the side of the road. Gabe drove alongside slowly.

Damn, it was cold outside. She paused and he stopped rolling forward. With a sigh she climbed back in the car. "Take me to Cooper's."

"Come with me to the hotel," Gabe said.

"I don't know what put your boxers in such a knot, but

I'm not going anywhere with you except to my brother's." She was shivering uncontrollably, and Gabe reached for her hands. Avoiding them, she rubbed her arms through her coat. "Was it because I was talking about my project to those men? You do realize I've been doing that for months now, right? It doesn't mean I'm going to sleep with them."

"No. Maybe it got to me a little, but I know you weren't flirting."

"So what? What is your problem? That I said I love you for talking to the mayor for me? I say I love you to Abby all the time. She knows it doesn't mean I'm asking her for a commitment." Men were so touchy about feelings. God. Give her girlfriends anyday.

"No."

"Then what?" It had to be the pictures. She would fix it. "If it's the photos, I'm really sorry. I had no idea—"

"Both the mayor and your friend recognized me from the Internet. For helping with your project. I don't know if you fully understand what this means for me, but if the wrong people see those pictures..." His knuckles were white on the steering wheel.

"I'm really sorry. I thought I told the knitting ladies, and then you did the hugs stand, but you told everyone your name." Her voice caught and she couldn't continue. Guilt flooded her. She had to find a way to take them down. "I'm sorry."

"Me too."

"So, you aren't freaked out that I said I might love you?"

"Do you think you love me?" He practically bit out the words.

She went cold all over again at his voice. Low and dangerous.

"Of course not. I was just happy you managed to get the

file to the mayor."

"Good." He drove, eyes fixed on the headlight beams shining on the black pavement.

Tears prickled in Lauren's eyes and she couldn't breathe very well.

"Take me home to Cooper's," she said, choking through the tight ring around her throat. "I'll stay there tonight."

Chapter 18

Lauren asked Gabe to drop her off at the corner so she could walk a block to her brother's house and he wouldn't see them together.

There was nothing to see, anyway.

Gabe had gotten what he wanted from her. And she had screwed him over by letting photos leak onto the Internet.

She was a naïve fool to think any arrangement they worked out would be for something more than sex. Time to pull up her big-girl panties and face reality.

No emotions. No entanglements. No complications.

She sat alone in her brother's living room until past midnight, drinking red wine and crying slow, fat tears. Gabe wasn't coming back to comfort her.

***

Gabe shouted several obscenities and hit the steering wheel the moment Lauren walked away from the car toward the house, but he didn't go after her. Knowing photos of him in stripper pants and eggnog body oil were posted all over the

Internet had his blood boiling too much to talk.

He needed a drink. He needed to be with other men and get her out of his head. Calling Cooper, he turned the car around and headed for town. The bar around the corner had exactly what he wanted—cheap whiskey.

Oddly enough, Cooper answered the phone when Gabe called him. "Yeah, man?"

"Don't tell me you're busy. I need a drink. Meet me at Murphy's as soon as you can."

"I'm already there."

The second he walked in the bar, he began to unwind. This was where he belonged, where he was supposed to be. He was single and intended to stay that way. Who needed relationships, sacrifices, long-distance drives and commitments? Not he.

He ordered a whiskey and found Cooper in the back around a pool table with a group of friends. A couple of girls he didn't recognize were there as well, drinking beer and joking. A blonde tipped her bottle his way and smiled in invitation. He nodded but didn't approach her. The last thing he needed was another woman in his life.

"You look like shit," Cooper said by way of greeting.

"Yeah?" Gabe asked. "You look like shit too." It was true. Cooper was haggard and unshaven, his work shirt wrinkled and hanging loose.

"I have a good reason. You?"

"Good enough." He drank his whiskey in one gulp and asked if anyone wanted anything from the bar.

"I'll have another of these," the blonde said, shaking her empty beer bottle.

"I'll have whatever you had. You up for the next game?" Cooper asked. He was setting the balls on the table.

"I hope you are." The blonde fondled a cue stick. "I'm

playing this round." She tossed her long hair over one shoulder, her tight top showing off her impressive curves.

If Gabe changed his mind about not having a woman in his life, he could have a guest warming his hotel bed.

"Sounds good. Be right back," he said.

An hour of playing pool and talking passed in a blur. After a few more whiskeys, Gabe couldn't remember anyone's name but his own and Cooper's, but it didn't seem important. The blonde was content to flirt and rub on him each time they got close, even going so far as to stroke his beard and lean her breasts on his arm while checking a shot he had lined up. Definitely no need to be lonely tonight.

"So what happened with your hookup?" Cooper asked when the girl was out of hearing.

"It's done and gone," he muttered, hitting two striped balls into the corner pocket, sharp *cracks* sounding through the room.

"Doesn't look like you're grieving much." Cooper chuckled. "So what was her name?"

"What kind of gentleman would I be if I told you?"

"All right. Out of curiosity, have you seen my sister lately? I haven't seen her in several days. She didn't even come home last night."

Gabe made a wild shot and nearly sank the eight ball. Damn. "I haven't seen her for a while, no." *I wish I were with her right now.*

"Yeah. I know she keeps busy between her job and that fundraiser thing. I don't know where she finds the energy to do both. She's too good for this town, if you ask me." Cooper edged along the side of the table to decide on his next move.

Blondie was practically blowing on Gabe's neck, giving him all sorts of ideas, and he felt himself tearing into two parts. Or maybe more.

"Proud of your little sister, aren't you?" Gabe said. His mouth had gone dry, and he wished he had a glass of water.

"Yeah, she's worlds better than I am, than you or anybody else I know. Except my momma, of course." Cooper grinned and took his shot, sinking the number six. He moved for the next one.

"Too good for any of your friends, in any case."

"You got that right." Cooper took another shot, sinking two.

Blondie made an impatient sigh. Apparently she was being neglected. Too bad.

"I was wondering," Gabe continued. "Why the shelter? Didn't you tell me once she was afraid of dogs?" It wasn't true, but he didn't know how else to bring up the subject. It had been bothering him since they ran into Aunt Jo and her dog, Ralphie, in the park. Why would a girl terrified of dogs spend so much time and energy trying to help them?

"I told you about how she was attacked by a stray when she was little? Yeah, she's been scared out of her mind of them ever since. It's such a pain when our aunt has us over for her family get-togethers. I swear she forgets to lock up her dog every single time."

"So why the shelter? Why not some other project?"

"I don't know. You'd have to ask her. That's who she is, though. She'd give the shirt off her back to anyone who needs it and never stop to think of herself. Drives my parents batshit. Do you know she spent her entire income for the month of November on a publicity drive for her fundraiser because she couldn't stand to use a dime of the money they had already gotten? This is a girl who needs new tires for her car."

Why would she do that?

Gabe couldn't recall ever meeting a girl who wasn't more

interested in shoes or a new dress than just about anything else.

A new dress. She didn't even buy a dress for herself to crash the mayor's party and Gabe had been an asshole about it.

But why an animal shelter? And when would Miss Blonde stop blowing on his ear?

"Hey, I think I'm going to take off." Gabe set his cue stick in the rack. The blonde winked at him.

"If you're going back to the house, I'll see you in a half hour or so. I think some of the guys are coming over for last drinks too," Cooper said.

A half hour wasn't much time, but it would have to suffice. It would be long enough to do what he needed to do. Blondie followed him from the back room.

"Hey, Gabe!" Cooper called. "If you see my sister, tell her I'll be home soon, all right?"

***

Lauren had just put the empty wine bottle in the kitchen and was weaving unsteadily across the living room when she heard a car arrive outside and a door slam. The car drove off.

Must have been the neighbors. She hated that two more tears welled up in her eyes and slid down her face. She was a mess tonight, and she was going to regret that bottle tomorrow.

The front door lock snicked, and in stepped Gabe, covered in a fine powder of snow. Frosty air gusted into the living room until he shut the door behind him.

"Hi." She reached toward her tear-and-mascara-streaked face to wipe her cheeks, thinking the bun she had made in her hair with a pencil must look like a bird's nest, but it was too late to do anything about it now. He had seen her. He was staring at her with a rather horrified expression, in fact. "I was just going to bed. I warmed up one of the seats on the sofa for you. Good night." The house was freezing inside again, since her brother had reset the thermostat. Tonight was not only going to be lonely, but damn cold.

"Lauren, wait," he called after her.

She got to her bedroom and shut the door in his face. She didn't need a pity party in her honor.

"Lauren, open up," he asked, knocking softly.

"Why?"

"So we can talk. I have to ask you something very important."

Leaning against the door, she rubbed her forehead on its cool surface and let it support her for a moment. The room was spinning, spinning, spinning round and round. A whole bottle might have been a bit much, even if she did eat olives and cheesy bread while drinking.

Wait. Something important? The pictures? Or maybe he was sorry for being a jerk after the mayor's party. A girl could dream.

She cracked open the door. His green eyes captured hers, not moving. Her heart did a little skipping jump and, unable to stop herself, she let him in the room.

"Is it about the photos? Because I am deeply, deeply sorry. I really thought I asked the ladies not to post anything."

"The pictures aren't your fault. It's my fault. I should have frisked those old women for phones. I might never work again, but that was the risk I took."

Maybe he'd said it to make her feel better, but he might as well have poured a bucket of tar on her head. "Then why are you here?"

He stuffed his hands in his jeans, hunching his shoulders. "I have to ask you, Lauren, why, um…why did you decide to raise money for a new animal shelter?"

Her jaw dropped in surprise. His important question was straight out of an interview for a middle school's monthly newsletter. Wait. She smelled alcohol—whiskey—on him. He had been drinking. The car she'd heard outside was a taxi driving him home from some bar.

"Because I wanted to. Bye." She motioned for him to leave.

"No, it's really important I understand. I know you're afraid of dogs, and you need to buy new tires, and you could get a date with any of those rich assholes checking you out tonight, but you are here alone instead. Why the animal shelter?"

"You aren't making any sense." He was drunk as a skunk. Or maybe she was. The room was still spinning pretty fast. She sat on the bed. It felt so good, she lay down looking up at the ceiling.

Gabe leaned over her, blocking her view of the drywall.

"You could have chosen another project. You could have a normal job doing nothing important. You could go on a date with Mr. Carter from Carter and Sons and have him buy you dresses and shoes. Why are you working so hard to save these animals if you don't even like them?"

"Who says I don't like them?"

"You are terrified of dogs."

"One bit me when I was five. A stray in the park. I'm lucky the scars faded." The nightmares had faded, too, but hadn't disappeared. She covered her face with her hands and felt Gabe crawl on the bed to straddle her. He lifted her hands away from her eyes.

"You would fight to save something that hurt you?"

"It was a stray. After it bit me, the pound put it to sleep. If it had been in loving home with owners, it never would have bit me and it wouldn't have been killed. Just because I'm afraid of dogs and don't like cats doesn't make it all right for me to stand by and let them suffer."

"And?"

What else did he want from her? "This is what I do to set things right. When you do something good, it makes it tougher for bad things to happen."

"Damn it, Lauren, you're so beautiful. You are making this so hard for me."

"Who said life was easy, Gabe?" she asked. "Besides, why should what I look like matter?"

"Not the outside of you, although you are damn irresistible, but the inside. If you were a shallow idiot, I wouldn't be having any problems."

"I'm so sorry," she said, rolling her eyes. The room flip-flopped. "If only I was a moronic slob, think of how great the casual Christmas sex would be."

"I didn't say the sex wasn't great."

She stopped being annoyed as a flutter of anticipation raced through her. Evil little butterflies. She would drown them all with more wine if she could stand.

"I was trying to say it's hard for me not to want more."

"After getting mad at me at the mayor's party for wearing the only dress I could find and drumming up support for my fundraiser, what makes you think you are ever getting more?"

"Because I'll explain I was a jealous jerk who couldn't stand the sight of other men ogling you and ask you to forgive me."

She grabbed his sweater and pulled him down for a hard kiss. He responded in kind, hands diving under her neck and shoulders to lift her upward. Tongues clashed and their breath mixed as they kissed in fierce hunger. He tasted like whiskey—smoky and dark.

She broke it off, pushing his chest. "You are not forgiven."

"If I go on my knees, would that make a difference?" Gabe knelt in front of her. He began to draw her sweatpants down over her hips.

She let him. Then he took off her panties. She shivered in the cold air right up to the moment Gabe made a line of kisses going up her inner thigh. Then she shivered with desire.

Farther off, the front door opened and the house flooded with the sounds of male voices laughing and talking. Boots stamped in the entryway and moved to the living room.

"My brother!" she hissed, twisting away and grabbing for her pants. Cooper's timing was the spawn of the devil. "You can't be in here!"

Gabe groaned. "Yeah, I know."

"Wait here and I'll see if they go in the kitchen," she said.

Someone knocked at her door.

"Are you in there, Lauren?" Cooper called.

"Uh, yeah, just a second." She spun toward Gabe. "Get in the closet."

"The closet? Are you—?"

She put a finger to his lips to shush him. "Closet. Now." She shoved him inside the tiny space.

Chapter 19

Lauren rubbed her face and patted her hair. The pencil had fallen out somewhere. She used the doorframe to hold herself upright and opened the door. "Hey, bro. What's up?"

"Not much, I…have you been crying?" Cooper asked, squinting.

"I was reading a documentary. I mean a biography. It was really sad. A woman had five kids who died of yellow fever. It was a long time ago. What's up with you?"

"Are you sure? Listen, there was something weird with Gabe this evening. He came to Murphy's and asked a couple of questions about you. It occurred to me that you were both gone last night, but when I asked him how his hookup was going, he said it was done. I just wanted to make sure he hadn't tried anything with you. Especially since he was hanging on a blonde at the bar. I would totally have to kick his ass."

"He had a blonde…as in a girl at the bar?" She was definitely going to kick his ass now. And then leave him naked and crying in the snow.

"Yeah, they left together. You didn't see him here

tonight?" Cooper asked.

"Um, nope, not tonight. Not last night, either. I was at Abby's, and we had a thing for the fundraiser earlier. I'm done until after Christmas now. Don't let your friends stay the night, okay? There's no room, and I don't want Dexter getting in bed with me."

"He wouldn't dare. He's afraid of me. You're sure you're all right? You look awful."

"Thanks, Cooper, right back at you. I think I need sleep more than anything else."

He nodded and began to go.

"Oh, and Coop? You don't have to worry about Gabe trying anything with me. I wouldn't touch him with Santa's sleigh."

Whatever that meant. She was seriously considering smacking him with Santa's whip. The nerve. Hanging on a blonde at the bar and then coming here to seduce her by asking for forgiveness. Not a chance. The blonde must not have worked out and he wanted some action tonight. Well, she wasn't going to give it to him.

"See you tomorrow, sis," Cooper said, waving good night.

She shut the door and locked it.

The closet creaked open slowly and Gabe poked his head out. "It's not at all how he made it sound."

She growled, an animalistic noise, and threw a pillow at him. "How was it, in that case? I hope you had fun."

"No, I didn't do anything at all with her. She was flirting while I was having some drinks. I wasn't interested."

"And that's why you left with her?"

"I didn't leave with her. She followed me—"

"I'm not hearing this." She jumped on the bed, needing very much to be taller than him. Being short and foaming-at-the-mouth furious was hard. "You were getting into my panties not one minute ago. Have you no shame?" She shoved him hard in the chest.

"She tried to follow me and I sent her home in a taxi. Alone. Alone, I swear."

"How can I believe you? Cooper saw you hanging on her."

"Lauren," he said, "I didn't touch her. It's true she was coming on to me while we were playing pool, but I put an end to it before anything happened. I came straight here, alone, from the bar." Hands up in the universal symbol of surrender, he stepped to the bed.

"How can I trust you?" she asked, throwing another pillow at him, surrender or no.

"You can't. Unless you choose to trust me. I was asking about you, I was thinking about you, I was wishing I was with you all evening. I tried to convince myself that being on my own was fun and having some random chick flirt with me was great, but...no. It wasn't. I had to come here to talk to you."

"And ask me about the animal shelter?"

He shrugged. "I know it sounds weird, but I had to know. I want to understand you. I want to get into every single part of your heart and mind and see what holds you together. I need every part of you."

It didn't sound weird, it sounded too good to be true. He needed every part of her. Holy sleigh bells ringing. She hesitated, breathing fast. "Do you need me because the blonde didn't pan out or because I'm raising money for animals I'm afraid of?"

"I need you because you are you."

His words went straight to her heart and filled it to the brim. She dropped the last pillow. Jumping on him, she wrapped her legs around his waist as he caught her. Her lips smashed against his. He stepped backward, bumping the nightstand into the wall before it wobbled on its three legs and fell with a thump.

Lauren heard it distantly but was too busy kissing Gabe and pulling at his clothes. She couldn't get enough of his lips and the rough scrape of his beard on her cheeks.

Steps came hurrying down the hall. Cooper banged on the door "Hey, are you all right in there?"

She jerked her head up, the room tilting dangerously. "Yes, everything's fine."

Gabe set her on the floor.

What had happened? The nightstand. "I bumped the nightstand and it fell. Everything's fine. Just a glass or two too many of red wine."

"Are you sure? Can I come in?"

She heaved a sigh. Her brother was a worrywart at the worst times. She waved frantically for Gabe to get back in the closet.

"I'm getting ready for bed. See you tomorrow," she called.

"Lauren, you didn't hit your head, did you? I had a friend who died like that," he said. It was a true a story.

"Go," she told Gabe. "Get in there, now!"

As soon as Gabe was safely hidden away in her closet again, she went to the door.

"I'm fine. I bumped my rear end, not my head. See, the table fell, but nothing's broken."

Cooper peeked inside, glancing from left to right. He set the table on its legs, picking the lamp up off the floor as well. "How much wine did you drink? There's an empty bottle on the counter."

"Then why are you asking me? There's an empty bottle on the counter." She shook her head. "You know. It was one of those evenings. The biography I read really got to me."

"Liar. It's some guy, isn't it?" He crossed his arms, leaning against the wall.

She prayed Gabe didn't have to sneeze.

"You can't hide him from me forever," Cooper said. "I can see things aren't going well. Is he mistreating you? Being an asshole? You say the word and I'll take care of him for you. I swear he'll never touch you again."

"I promise there isn't a guy. I am not hiding anyone. Anywhere. From you."

Especially not in my closet.

"If you say so." He pushed off the wall. "Sleep tight."

She locked the door behind him and pressed her ear to the wood. When her brother's footsteps faded down the hallway, she returned to the closet.

"You might have to sleep in here tonight," she said with another sigh. Her face was numb from the wine and from Gabe's insistent kissing earlier. Tomorrow would be hell. "I don't know how to sneak you to the living room without him finding out."

Gabe pulled her into the closet and shut the door.

***

"A bottle's worth of red wine, huh?" Gabe asked. He couldn't take advantage of a drunk girl. She listed sideways and he wrapped his arms around her. "In that case, we'll have to be good and just sleep."

"In the closet?"

"No, I want a good-night kiss. Then, I'll wait for your brother to go to bed and stage my return home." He placed a few chaste kisses strategically on her cheeks and jaw.

She breathed in and out deeply, melding her body into his. "Just one good-night kiss?"

"Maybe a couple. But you've been hitting the sauce a bit hard, so after that it's off to bed with you." Unfortunately.

"Out of curiosity, how much whiskey did you have?"

"Enough."

"So much you couldn't drive yourself home?"

He ran kisses down her neck. "It was safer to take a taxi. I stopped counting shots after three."

"I think that makes us even, in that case," she said. "You can go ahead and take advantage of me."

"I shouldn't. It wouldn't be gentlemanly." His lips were on her collarbone, and he licked the delicate triangle of skin at the base of her throat.

"I think you should. Remember what happened in the last closet? Now it's my turn." She traced circles on his stomach under his shirt.

Last closet? His mind churned sluggishly to recall. Right before the mayor's party... His cock, already at half-mast, came fully to life and pushed hard against his jeans. "We should wait for tomorrow when we can go back to the hotel."

"I dare you."

Her breath tickled his ear, sending a streak of heat to his balls. "You dare me to do what?"

"I dare you to go down on me in this closet. Don't expect me to double dare you, either. My dare, your turn."

He didn't have the strength to resist her insistence. In the near-darkness of the closet, he went to his knees, pulling her sweatpants down as he lowered himself. He put her leg over his shoulder, then ran his tongue and lips up her inner thigh.

She moaned softly.

He kissed his way closer to her sex and the soft curls that hid it.

She moaned louder.

Thank you, Cooper, for inviting your friends over. No fucking way was anyone going to hear her over the rowdy voices and laughter from the kitchen.

Gabe moved deeper to suck on her clit, finding it swollen

from their brief encounter earlier.

"Don't stop until I finish, that's the dare," she reminded him.

He had to grin to himself. He had no intention of stopping. He used his tongue to lightly skim her sex, teasing at the entrance and against her clit. She fisted his hair.

He pressed harder with his tongue, moving rhythmically and listened for her breathing to increase. He was rewarded with a gasp. He could continue this all night, he decided. Who needed sleep?

"Gabe, I want…" She sounded desperate.

He slid two fingers into her and back out, letting her bucking hips and inarticulate noises tell him to go faster or slower.

She was sweet and salty, and he was lost in the incredible sensation of enhancing her pleasure. He held on tight to her leg and waist as she pressed against the wall. Her skin was slick under his hands as she broke into a fine sweat. He swirled his tongue hard on her clit and she gasped loudly.

"Yes, like that." She dug her fingers into his shoulders and rocked against him.

He worked her harder and faster, not relenting with his mouth or fingers, and she panted in response. He wanted to feel her come.

She began to shake, and he had to support her from collapsing against the wall.

"Gabe," she called through clenched teeth. The waves of her orgasm slowed and she relaxed against him.

Sitting back on his heels, he let her fall into his lap, crushing his erection. She laid her head on his shoulder, totally spent. Or so he thought.

"I need you to fuck me now."

"Fuck you now?" His resolve to not take advantage of her

while she was drunk was fading fast.

"Right now." She unsnapped his pants.

He raised her so he could slide them over his erection. The second it sprang free, she was lowering herself onto him. The feeling of her warm, wet sex sliding down his bare skin was indescribable, and he bucked involuntarily, ramming her to the hilt.

Her lips came down to his while he continued to thrust inside her, despite the awkward position. Their shirts were still on, and he pulled at hers, wanting her naked breasts on his chest. She helped him as she rode him, the walls of her sex tight around his erection. Her shirt came off and he took one breast in his mouth, sucking at her nipple.

He wasn't going to last much longer. Waves of pleasure crashed into him, and he felt the need to thrust even harder.

"Hold on to me," he ordered, and she wrapped her legs and arms around him.

He carried her from the closet and dropped her on the bed. Standing at its edge, he flipped her over to her knees in front of him. "You want this?" he asked, voice ragged and edged with desire. He stood at her entrance and traced a line down her spine to her perfect ass.

"Yes."

He thrust into her, shaken hard to the core with his need. No one had ever driven him this wild with lust before. The only thing that existed at that moment was her luscious body moving with his.

She had to bury her head in a pillow to cover her cries as she called out with pleasure during her orgasm.

When it hit, his orgasm rippled through him in powerful shocks that nearly brought him to his knees behind her. From deep in his center, pleasure coursed upward and out, flowing through him as he emptied himself in her. Catching his breath as the aftershocks slowed and eased, he pulled out. He stretched out flat on the bed, drawing her close to put her head on his chest, probably more content than he'd ever been.

It took several minutes before he felt the cold in the room. Time to get under the covers.

"Tell me we can still see each other after Christmas," he whispered. He shifted some to grab the blankets. "This is too good to end tomorrow. We can keep this going as long as you want."

She sat up suddenly, facing him, horror written on her face.

"We forgot to use a condom."

Chapter 20

Lauren vowed she would never drink another sip of alcohol so long as she was single for the rest of her life.

"It's okay," Gabe said. "I'm clean. I'm sure you're clean. There are products at the pharmacy for—"

"Shhh!" She rolled out of bed, scrambling for her clothes. "I can't believe I did that. I can't believe you didn't remember. And yes, I'm clean, but shit! I can't believe this."

"Lauren," he said, taking her arms and forcing her to face him. "It's all right."

"For who? It's all right for you? I can't take this anymore. One minute one of us is mad at the other, the next we're having sex. You drive me crazy." She couldn't stay in the room with him any longer.

"Where are you going?"

"To take a shower or something. I have to think. I can't...I can't be like this with you." She left him in the spare bedroom while she tiptoed across the hall to the bathroom.

Running hot water on her head and stiff shoulders helped calm her down. She must be insane. She had never let a boyfriend forget to wear a condom before. The worst part was how good it felt. How free and wonderful—the way it should be if you loved someone and were in a committed relationship. But that wasn't the case and it wouldn't be the case with Gabe.

He lived in Boston. Hours and hours away. At best he'd get that job in Richmond, although it seemed highly unlikely. Stupid pictures. She knew for a fact she couldn't move away from her family and Sycamore Cove. She'd tried it already.

This was just a Christmas-vacation thing. Casual, mind-blowing sex for a few days and then back to the tedious ho-hum of real life.

She took her time scrubbing and soaking in the downpour. Not that she felt the urge to be cleaned of Gabe or his touch on her skin, but the water's warmth was comforting. She had to face the truth. He would be gone soon and it was best they severed their contact.

Mind made up, she dried herself off, pulled on a clean set of pajamas, and left the bathroom.

The party had died in the meantime, and Cooper's door was shut. Snoring rumbled softly from his room. Gabe stepped into view from the living room.

"Listen, there is nothing you have to deal with alone." He reached to take her in his arms, but she shrugged him off. "We'll handle this however you want. I can take you to the—"

"I think it's best if I take care of things tomorrow. I'll go to the pharmacy and see what they have. It's early in the month for my cycle, so I'm sure there's nothing to worry about."

"Whatever happens, we'll figure it out together."

"When? When you're back in Boston?" she asked, heading for her room.

He grabbed her hand to stop her. "Just because I'm

leaving doesn't mean we have to end things or pretend nothing ever happened. We can still be together."

"I don't think I can take any more of this. Didn't I already say that?" she asked. "Don't you see that since we met, like five days ago, it's been back and forth, up and down, and total madness? You drive me crazy."

"You drive me crazy too. What we have is amazing."

"What we have? And what is that exactly?"

"Incredible chemistry for starters. This thing between us is the most fun I've ever had."

"'Fun'? Yeah, it's all just fun and games for you, isn't it? Well, that's all it was for me, too, but it's over and you are leaving. Good night." She moved past him without touching him and shut herself in her room. For the second time that night, huge tears filled her eyes and streamed down her face. When did this become so difficult?

Why did doing the right thing instead of making another mistake have to punch a hole in her chest?

The next morning, she rose early out of habit. Reindeer must have trampled her brain during the night. Neither Gabe nor Cooper were awake when she left the house.

It was Christmas Eve and she was going to the pharmacy for a morning-after pill. The fear she might get pregnant effectively obliterated any holiday cheer she would normally drum up. Next year, she was going on a cruise to the Caribbean if she had to sell a kidney. Her mom and stepdad must be having such a great time. And she couldn't even call her mom without ruining it for her.

A very Merry Christmas, everybody.

The pharmacist explained how to take the medication and recommended she take it with food.

That meant she had to go to Les Amis for coffee and croissants. It was a short but difficult drive to the restaurant.

Last-minute shoppers scurried to and fro, crossing streets and smiling and waving at each other. So happy. So busy getting ready for see the family and give gifts.

With her mother and stepfather away, she only had presents for Cooper and her aunt, and little gifts from flea markets for her friends and committee helpers. She was done shopping. Parking Cooper's car at Les Amis, she stared at the dusty dashboard.

No dashing or prancing or bushels of fun for her this year. Gabe left in a day or two, and that was it.

She didn't have a present for him.

Jiminy Christmas. She kicked herself. He had gotten plenty from her—more than he deserved.

The interior of Les Amis welcomed her like a season's greetings postcard, and she warmed at the familiarity. This was home as much as her mom's house was. Isabelle even hugged her as she rushed by, busy as could be in the morning.

He was there. Gabe sat in a booth, facing the door at the back. He saw her come in and pointed at the plate in from of him.

She shook her head in disbelief.

He beckoned her closer, holding the plate up so she could see what it held. Damn. Tempted by a cinnamon bun. In a way, he was still playing games, and as usual she was unable to resist. She caved, collapsing in the seat opposite him.

A french press carafe of coffee was on the table, too, waiting for her. Maybe he wasn't so bad after all. But they couldn't continue seeing each other.

"Morning," he said. His wide hands were wrapped around a mug full of coffee, and she poured a cup for herself.

"Morning." Inhaling the coffee aroma deeply, she closed her eyes a moment. Why couldn't they keep seeing each other? Long distance wasn't the end of the world. She set the pill on the table.

"Whatever happens, I am with you," he said.

She took his glass of water to swallow the little pill. He passed the milk and sugar for her coffee. He already knew how she liked it.

"How did you know I would be here?" she asked.

"You get free croissants and coffee, and cinnamon buns according to Isabelle. Why would you go anywhere else?" He paused, watching her. "I didn't just come to chat, though. Something came up and I need to show you a place here in town."

"'Something came up'? What do you mean?"

"There's a place we have to go to," was his cryptic reply.

"All right. But there aren't many nooks or crannies of this town I haven't seen."

"Yeah. There is this one place. Not really a shop, more of an old building I need to take you to visit."

"Which old building?" The library, city hall, or perhaps another place here in the historical town square? Not much was open on Christmas Eve besides shops and churches, and Gabe wanting to go last-minute sightseeing didn't mesh with the little she knew of him.

"You and I are going to visit the animal shelter."

She went cold. The bite of cinnamon bun in her mouth turned to tasteless mush. "No, I don't think so."

"I called them and they are thrilled you'll be stopping by for the first time ever. They love you, you know. The lady on the phone loves me, too, since I got five kittens adopted the evening of the bake sale, but she loves you more."

"Gabe, try to understand. I am terrified of dogs. It isn't rational. It isn't healthy. But it is real."

"Listen, I didn't want it to come to this, but I have another card to play if necessary."

Now she remembered. Games. He was always playing. This was why they couldn't keep seeing each other. "I know everything's a game to you, but don't waste your time on this. I don't care if you dare me, because I won't go."

"Lauren." He placed his hand on hers. It was hot from the cup of coffee but sent chills through her fingers into her heart. "They have a letter from the mayor and they want to give it to you personally."

Nothing short of angels showing up and playing trumpets could have made her stand faster.

She grabbed her phone, wrapped the cinnamon bun in a napkin, and gulped the hot coffee. "All right, let's go."

They headed to Gabe's car. She was shaking too much to drive.

"How do you know about the letter?" she asked.

He fished in his coat pocket, steering with one hand. "You left your phone at the house, and I heard them calling several times. Here."

"You answered my phone?" There it was in his hand. She took it and swiped to check the call history.

"No. When I noticed they tried a couple of times, I called them to ask if they wanted me to get ahold of you and give you a message. The lady was only too happy to have my assistance. A real chatty Cathy. I know the history of her family, the animal shelter, the lives of the people working there, and how the mayor himself came this morning to deliver the letter. It's addressed to you, so she doesn't know what it says."

"Oh my God. Can you drive faster?"

"Not on this ice."

"Turn left at the light," she said. "Didn't you say he seemed pretty negative at the party? What if he says no?"

"What if he says yes?"

She bit her lower lip and pressed both hands against the dashboard to stay calm. The mayor had an answer. He had gone through the file last night and made up his mind. Another five minutes to go, that was all. Somehow, she kept from shouting as Gabe drove.

But the second they arrived at the shelter, her body stopped obeying her. She held the car door handle and frowned at the single-story building as she took in its rusty chain-link fence, crumbling bricks, small windows, and sagging front steps. It was too horrible. Not even the heavy snow covering it, the plastic reindeer out front, or Santa climbing up the side helped her.

Dogs barked loudly inside.

Fear as strong as iron and cold as ice gripped her chest, and for a moment, she couldn't breathe. She forced herself out of the car, but her legs wobbled and her hands trembled. Her whole body shook. She couldn't go in there. Images that haunted her dreams throughout her entire childhood crashed into her mind: a dog's snapping jaws, slobber on yellow fangs, the pain shooting up her arm, and her own screams drowning every other sound around her.

"Lauren!"

Her parents had yelled her name as they ran across the playground. They were yelling and she was screaming, but the pain wouldn't stop and the dog wouldn't let go.

"Lauren!"

Gabe had her in his arms. She wasn't screaming. She didn't feel any pain. She wrapped her arms around him, squeezing as tight as she could. He would keep her safe.

"Hey," he said, getting her attention, "it's all right. It's all right. I know you're scared, but you have to listen to me. I'm going to ask you to just to hear me out. Yeah?"

She nodded, thankful she could breathe again and the

memory of the dog was fading as long as she could focus on Gabe.

"I don't know anything about trauma or panic attacks, but I did see you in the park when your aunt showed up with her furry mutt in tow, and also with the puppy at the bake sale. Remember?"

She nodded some more. How could she forget?

"You were scared then, too, but you kept it under control. I believe if you know consciously that you're safe, then unconsciously you're able to keep the fear at bay. I know this'll be hard, but it would mean so much to the people who work here for you to walk through those doors and greet them and the animals. You have to believe you're safe."

"How the hell do you know all that? You can't be sure. What if I have a breakdown? What if I spend Christmas in the mental hospital?" No way was she walking into that building.

"The simple fact you can ask those questions tells me you'll be fine. I'm not saying it will be easy, but you can do this."

More cars pulled into the small parking area, and people from her fundraising committee piled out. They called her name and practically jumped for joy. They wanted her to go inside to read the mayor's letter.

She nodded at them, too, beginning to feel like a windup doll. Nod, wave, take a few steps in a circle. Repeat.

Aunt Jo drove up and parked in the street, and Cooper stepped out of the passenger side. Lauren jumped away from Gabe as if he'd burned her. Gabe took a deep breath, dropping his arms, but didn't react otherwise.

Committee members milled around her, waiting for her to make the first move toward the door. Her stomach bottomed out and she knew she was going to be sick within thirty seconds. Give or take five.

Abby burst out of the building, shouting her name.

"Lauren, what are you doing out here? Santa has come and gone early, girl! Now let's see what he left us!" She grabbed Lauren's hand and tugged. Lauren's feet might as well have been nailed to the concrete.

"You are stronger than you think," Gabe said. "You are so much stronger than your fear when you let yourself be. Remember the snow-swimming dare? Just dive in."

She shot him a death-inducing glare, or so she hoped. "I remember it being cold as hell and absolutely horrible." But she let Abby pull her toward the building. She even managed to go up the two stairs to the front door.

Furious barking engulfed her and her knees buckled.

Chapter 21

Gabe saw Lauren pitching sideways and caught her.

"Lauren?" he asked, holding her arms.

Enough. It was too hard for her and strictly speaking, not necessary. So what if she had never stepped foot in the building? She was trying to get rid of it.

Her wide eyes met his when she looked for him and she smiled, reassured that he was there. This he could do. He could stand with her while she faced her fears.

She reached for the door and swung it wide, letting loose a cacophony of dogs barking, cats meowing, and birds chirping. Gabe suspected he could even hear a hamster wheel or two squeaking above the rest of the noise.

A grandmotherly lady with bright blue hair clapped her hands and pulled Lauren inside, first for a hug, then for a kiss on the cheek, and then another hug. This must be the receptionist. Blue suited her.

"Hi, Mildred," Lauren said, croaking froglike.

"I can't believe you're here, sweetheart," Mildred said. "You finally had a chance to say hi. Come and meet my babies."

Lauren swiveled to give him a terrified shake of the head, but the receptionist dragged her to the back before Gabe could save her. He followed. The rest of the group followed him.

Cooper caught up to him. "Where did you find her?" His voice was cold and sharp.

"Going for breakfast at the French place."

"You two are pretty friendly. What was that hugging in the parking lot all about?"

"Exactly what it looked like," Gabe wasn't going to be intimidated. "She was scared out of her mind and I hugged her. If we've gotten friendly during my stay, you've got yourself to blame. I've hardly seen you the whole time."

"And just how friendly are you two? Seriously. Did you try something with my little sister?"

"I wouldn't say I tried anything, no."

Cooper's face twisted in anger. "What exactly did you do?"

"That's between me and Lauren." He was ready when Cooper grabbed his shirt but not for the pure rage in his face. Cooper's fist came up.

"Quiet, everyone! The press is here," someone shouted.

The people in the crowded corridor and back room jostled to make space for the journalist and a cameraman, and the crush of bodies pushed Gabe and Cooper apart.

Gabe recognized Sandra from the bake sale, the black journalist with the legs that didn't end.

Sandra crinkled her brow when she saw him. "Gabe, nice to see you again. And...Cooper." She paused, dark eyes narrowing. "Thanks for the call. It's not often the mayor hand-delivers letters on Christmas Eve. This promises to be interesting."

Cooper coughed, tendons in his neck popping. "I thought

you would want to know. I wouldn't have bothered you otherwise."

"So where is Lauren Hall and this famous letter?" she asked the group.

A scared peep carried over the barking, and everyone turned to face a pale, trembling Lauren. She stood in the middle of two rows of dog pens, her arms pinned to her sides, eyes darting back and forth between caged dogs. They barked and wagged tails, gnawing at the bars. There was even a very slobbery pug trying frantically to lick his way to freedom.

Lauren seemed about two seconds away from fainting. He tried to reach her, but the receptionist was closer.

Mildred handed Lauren an envelope, placing her plump arm around her shoulders.

Lauren's hand shook, and she turned it over a couple of times, reading and rereading her name written in heavy, black ink. Gabe maneuvered as close as possible, while Sandra and her cameraman set up the shot and asked if Lauren was ready.

"Yes," she said in a breathy voice. "I hope the mayor has some good news for us. As you can see, the dogs are not very comfortable in their old crates."

"Go on and open it," Sandra encouraged her. The whole room hushed in anticipation. Even the dogs were quieter, pacing in their tiny living spaces.

Lauren tore open the envelop. She lifted the letter out and unfolded it slowly.

"He says…" She couldn't continue. Shining tears filled her eyes, and one escaped down her cheek. She shook her head. "He says he's sorry, but…"

"What?" several voices shouted. "Sorry?"

"How could he do this on Christmas?"

"Let her finish!"

Lauren held up her hand, shaking her head more. "Wait.

He says he's sorry, but construction on the new, no-kill-policy shelter won't be able to start until spring!" She was crying now. And laughing. "They'll start in the spring! We'll have a new shelter before the end of next year!" She clasped the letter to her chest.

Everyone whooped, shouting and hugging one another. The dogs went ballistic. They didn't know what everyone was celebrating, but they weren't picky. The noise was deafening. Abby grabbed Gabe for a big squeeze. Some guy from the committee gave him a hug. An old lady who looked like a knitter patted his butt and winked. Cooper glared at him.

The cameraman got it all on film. Sandra called Lauren's name, trying to get her attention and be heard over the ruckus.

***

"How does this make you feel?" Sandra yelled, holding the mic in Lauren's face.

"Wonderful! This is my Christmas present from Santa." She waved the letter. "The only thing on my wishlist this year." Or at least the only thing on her list before Gabe blew in with the snowstorm. One out of two Christmas wishes for her stocking would have to suffice.

"Can we get a shot of you with one of the dogs? How about it?"

The blood drained from Lauren's face. She shook her head.

Hold one of the dogs? The woman was obviously insane. Lauren stuttered, protesting, but Sandra wasn't taking no for an answer.

Mildred elbowed her way to Lauren's side.

"We certainly don't want to bother any of the animals," the receptionist said, coming between her and the journalist. "But this old sweetheart won't ever be adopted, and the only thing he wants to do is cuddle."

A hot ball of silky fur dropped into her arms, and she reflexively caught it. She could sense brittle bones under the fur, and a small, shaking Cocker Spaniel too old to do anything but wheeze curled up in her hold.

A grizzled snout emerged from the bundle, sniffing. Big, wet eyes stared and a bigger, wetter nose rubbed on her neck. Then the dog began to lick her.

It reminded her in a weird way of Gabe's kisses on her neck, and she let out a chuckle.

"Why won't he ever be adopted? He's so gentle," Lauren said.

"Too old. Families want young pets. His time would normally be up, but we've been delaying putting him to sleep, hoping the new shelter would be announced."

"I'll adopt him!" Aunt Jo cried from the crowd. "He's mine. I have first dibs!"

"Jo, he hates cats," Mildred said. The women started arguing and several other volunteers stepped forward to adopt the old canine.

Sandra began to interview another person, and Abby took the dog out of Lauren's arms.

"You did good," Abby said, winking.

Lauren sighed with relief. On the way out of the dog room, she paused at the last pen. A mixed breed was huddled in the far corner. His tangled, dirty fur and bony ribs told her exactly how he had been mistreated and abused.

It resembled the dog who had bitten her so long ago. She crouched at the bars, not too close.

"Hey, boy," she said. "We'll get you cleaned up and fed for Christmas, don't worry."

He whined and thumped his tail but didn't get up from the corner.

"Looks like he's had it pretty bad," Gabe said, coming to squat next to her. He called the dog softly, holding a treat through the bars. The dog pricked up his ears and sniffed, then climbed painfully to his feet and padded over. He gingerly took the dog biscuit, scarfing it down and hunching his back fearfully.

"He's more afraid of us than you are of him, that's for sure," Gabe said.

Lauren decided he had never looked sexier than there in the grungy room, trying to comfort both an abused dog and her at the same time.

He's leaving tomorrow and the fun and games are over.

The dog crept closer to lean against the bars, and Gabe stretched his fingers in to scratch him behind his ears. Lauren cautiously put in her fingers next to his and gave a quick scratch. Nothing bad happened. She smiled.

"You know you two are under the mistletoe, right?" Aunt Jo asked, appearing out of nowhere.

Lauren glanced up, and sure enough, a branch of mistletoe hung over their heads. They stood.

"Well, go on and kiss! You are the strangest couple I've ever met," Aunt Jo said.

Cooper walked up behind her.

Gabe shook his head. "We're just friends."

"You weren't just friends the other night in the gazebo. I never saw such a lip lock."

Cooper turned a dark shade of red. "That's it. Let's go." He grabbed for Gabe and Lauren jumped up.

"It's not like that. Nothing happened, Coop," she cried. She wedged herself between them, hands on Cooper's chest.

"No, bring it on, Cooper. You think I'm afraid?" Gabe yelled over her head.

Dogs were frantic, barking madly and the crowd of people

pressed to the walls of the reception area to get out of the way.

Sandra called out to her cameraman, "Are we still filming?"

He nodded, a donut in his mouth.

"This whole time, you've been trying to hook up with my sister." Spittle flew from Cooper's mouth. He held Lauren to the side. "With my little sister."

"I told you, I wasn't *trying* to do anything."

Cooper barreled into Gabe's chest, shoving him back into the reception counter.

Gabe grunted on impact, face blotched red. "She's a grown-up, man. She makes her own choices!"

"But that doesn't include dating your friends. You don't have to fight." Lauren yanked on Cooper's arm.

Gabe pushed off the counter, shoulder in Cooper's gut. They stumbled through the front door, down the stairs, and into a huge snowdrift, Lauren running after them.

Shelter employees, fundraiser committee members, friends, and the local news crew poured out of the building to see what would happen next.

Cooper shook snow from his face, trying to find his balance. He pointed at Gabe. "I will kick your ass from here to Boston. You were talking about her when you said you had a sure thing in town. My sister. Jesus. You treated her like a piece of garbage."

"He didn't treat me like that," Lauren protested.

Cooper wasn't listening. He swung for Gabe and they both went down in a tangle.

"And now what?" Cooper continued. "You aren't even together. She means nothing to you."

"That's not true." Gabe head-butted Cooper, and they were in the snow again.

"So you're dating, or what?" Cooper asked as they

wrestled. White powder flew in every direction and they were caked in it like Abominable Snowmen.

Lauren almost jumped in to separate the two, but she was afraid of getting hit in the crossfire of wild punches.

Gabe drew back, chest heaving. "It's complicated."

"Can we not talk about this now?" Lauren asked.

"Explain it to me." Cooper held up a hand to pause the fight.

Gabe gasped for breath a moment. "I told her she can come to Boston anytime she wants to see me. I've had the greatest time this trip. What we have going here is hot."

Lauren's hands flew to her mouth. Whatever he had should have said to placate Cooper, that wasn't it.

"The hell?" Cooper yelled. "Are you saying my sister is your long-distance booty call?" Without waiting for an answer, he tackled Gabe, driving him deep in the snow.

"'Booty'?" Aunt Jo asked her. "Is that like a pirate's treasure? I wouldn't mind being treated like a pirate's treasure by that redhead."

Abby snorted a laugh. "Yo ho ho and I'll bring the rum!"

"No, Aunt Jo, it's not pirate treasure." Lauren glared at her aunt and best friend.

"Miss Hall, can I ask how you feel about being referred to as a 'long-distance booty call' by your...should I say former lover?" Sandra asked, shoving the mic in Lauren's face.

"What? He didn't say...that was my brother who said...What do you mean 'former lover'?"

"So he's not your former lover? Should we understand that you two have an ongoing relationship? Did I hear correctly that he'll be returning to Boston soon?" Sandra asked.

Gabe fought his way up and stuffed snow down Cooper's shirt.

"John, you're getting all this, right?" Sandra asked her cameraman.

"Ooooh, yeah," he replied.

At that moment Lauren realized how hard up the newspeople were for entertainment. Nothing was going on in the whole county they would rather cover.

"Enough," she shouted, wading into the snow. "Stop right this instant, both of you!" She floundered until she reached them. "Cooper, stop. Please, just listen. Yes, things got a little warm between Gabe and I, but it's over. He's going back to Boston and I am staying here, and that's the end of it."

"You pile of shit." Cooper lunged weakly toward Gabe, who stumbled sideways.

"Stop, Cooper," she said.

"When you say 'warm,' Miss Hall, do you really mean hot?" Sandra asked, jumping in the snow with her.

Cooper rounded to face her, incredulous. "Not now, Sandra."

"Oh, sweetie. Paybacks are hell, aren't they?" Sandra patted his cheek.

"For once, I'm going to side with my brother. Can you save whatever personal issues you have with him for later? Preferably when he's the one being publicly humiliated?" Lauren asked.

"This is current events, but I'll try," Sandra said, sniffing. She pointed a french-manicured finger at the two men gasping for breath, their shirts hanging open and chests exposed to the frosty air. "Can we get a close-up on the torn shirts?"

For Sandra, it must have been a sexy, snowman WrestleMania with a bit of romantic drama sprinkled on top, but for Lauren it was a disaster. She clutched her head. This was her life.

"Cooper," she said, "it's no big deal. You don't have to pummel him. He's going home and that's the end of it."

"Fine. But you are not going up to Boston on the weekends. He can find some other chick to hook up with for his great time," Cooper said, slashing his hand downward as if heads were going to roll if she didn't agree with him.

"Fine. Show's over." Lauren slumped, suddenly exhausted as adrenaline drained from her muscles. She pretended that agreeing to never see Gabe again didn't break her heart when what she wanted to do was curl up on the ground like the abandoned dog in his crate.

"No, this is not over." Gabe stomped toward Lauren, Cooper coming for him at the same time.

Sandra backed away to not block the view and Lauren squeaked, falling on her ass in the snow.

"I've got one more dare," Gabe said, "and I'm using it now."

"No. No more dares. All of this has been a big game for you. Well, it's over."

"What's this about a game of dare?" Cooper asked. Sandra held him back, her hand on his shoulder.

"Dares?" Abby shouted from the sidelines. "You sly minx, you didn't tell me anything about dares!"

"Not everything is a game to me, Lauren," Gabe pulled her to standing, focusing intensely on her. "There's nothing fun about this. I have a confession of my own to make. I haven't told anyone, not my family or my friends, but I was laid off three weeks ago. Maybe I'll get the job I interviewed for in Richmond, but probably not. But everything I did—the cake, the elf costume, the hugs, and crashing the mayor's party, everything was worth it. It might cost me that job, and others, but it was worth it to be with you. There. I've said it. Now it's your turn."

She shook her head in confusion.

"I dare you to be honest with me, Lauren."

Chapter 22

Lauren grasped at his words, trying to make sense of them. He didn't have a job in Boston? Why would he spend so much on a hotel room for them? How could she be worth ruining his career?

She wasn't sure what Gabe was asking, either. Be honest? She was hiding her feelings a bit, but everything she said was true. The second he left Sycamore Cove, she wouldn't be seeing him anymore.

"I don't understand," she said.

"I dare you to be honest."

"I got that part, but I am honest," she said.

"I haven't heard you once say what you want. Not once. I haven't ever heard you being honest with your brother about what you want or who you are. It's not enough to pretend it doesn't matter. Stand up for yourself and tell me honestly what you want," he said. "I. Dare. You."

"You dare me to talk about my personal, private feelings in front of all these people, in front of a news camera? What kind of dare is that?"

"A necessary one. I'm going to leave soon, and you just told all these people it's fine with you if I go. You told your brother that what we did and what we had was no big deal and that it's over. Well, it's a big deal to me, believe it or not."

"Screw you, Gabe," she said. "This whole time, you're the one saying things like 'We should keep getting together even after Christmas,' and 'We can be discrete so your brother doesn't find out.'"

"I'm gonna kill you," Cooper muttered. "The second the camera goes off, you are dead."

"She has a point!" Abby suddenly chimed in. "The other day when she dropped the L-bomb, you totally froze up."

"What's the L-bomb?" Aunt Jo asked, terrified.

"Everyone else, stay out of this," Gabe said. "Lauren, I'm not saying I've been honest or perfect. Hell, I even blamed you for the pictures getting posted, but I need you to tell me what you want. Maybe I can give it to you and maybe I can't, but I have to know."

Silence fell over the crowd. A crow cawed in the distance.

"I can't do this," Lauren said. "Not here."

Cooper shoved his way to her side. "Let's go home."

"I double dare you," Gabe said. "Don't make me double-dog dare you."

"I can't have what I want," she said.

"But you can say it." He cupped her face so she had to look him in the eyes. "I triple-dog dare you."

The dare etiquette was off. But she couldn't say what was in her heart.

"Sure, you both can talk all you want. But what about the other girls I saw you with in town?" Cooper asked him. "Since we're being so open and honest here, tell us about them. I saw you talking with Shannon a couple of days ago, crowding up to breathe in her face, and last night you left the bar with that blonde. Gabe, you cannot stay faithful to one girl to save your life. Lauren is too good for you. Admit it and get the fuck out of here."

"She is too good for me, but I'm not leaving until she does this dare." He dropped his hands but remained focused on her, waiting.

Lauren could see Sandra motioning to John to do a close-up of her face. Abby was still whispering to Aunt Jo behind her, probably still explaining that *L-bomb* meant "love."

"What about the drunk blonde who was all over you at the bar?" Cooper asked.

"I put her in a taxi. What time did I leave the bar?"

"About midnight," Cooper answered.

"What time did I arrive at the house, Lauren?"

"It was a little after midnight," she said. "What day was he talking to Shannon?" she asked Cooper.

"A couple days ago. I had a thing in town and saw them together at the corner of Baker Street. They were talking, and she handed him something. It seemed like more than a friendly encounter to me."

"It was the day I found you at the boat show," Gabe told Lauren. "Remember? She gave me back my glove. You called her to dress up as Mrs. Claus. That's how I knew where you were. You remember that evening, right?"

"You met up with Lauren right after leaving some other chick?" Cooper paced, shaking his arms loose like a boxer gearing up for a fight.

"Lauren, you can trust me on this. I haven't been with anyone but you," Gabe said. "We saw her at the hotel that night. She rented us the suite."

"And she was mad to see you there with me," Lauren said.

"Because in town she had offered me a room. I'm sorry I didn't tell you. She thought I was there for her until you came out of the bathroom."

"How can I know for sure?" Lauren asked. "You want me to trust you and be honest and to lay my heart out on the line for everyone to see, but you haven't given me any good reasons to, and I don't even know if I can trust you."

"Call her."

"Who?"

"Shannon. Call her. Ask if anything happened between us. You can take my word for it or you can call her," Gabe said.

Cooper was fuming, red in the face, but Lauren was beginning to feel the cold. A terrible cold that spread from her heart outward. The friendship between Cooper and Gabe was destroyed, and it was her fault. The fragile connection between her and Gabe was about to snap as well. She took her phone from her pocket.

***

Gabe watched, holding his breath, as Lauren flipped through her contacts and found Shannon's number.

The crowd around them didn't make a peep as she waited for the other woman to answer.

For all Gabe knew, Shannon could be a vindictive witch. She could lie to Lauren for any number of reasons: to build up her own image, to be cruel to a rival, or just for the fun of it. Women were their own worst enemies sometimes.

"Hi, Shannon," Lauren said. "I'm sorry to bother you on Christmas Eve." She paused. "Oh, the suite was fine. Fabulous view. I have a strange question."

Cooper pointed at him upon hearing the word *suite*. He never thought his friend could be so furious. His guts churned in nervous agony. If he lost Lauren because of this....

"Do you remember Gabriel Nicholson? Yes. The ginger." She laughed nervously. "The evening we checked in was also the day I called asking if you could do the boat show and wear the Mrs. Claus outfit. I think you saw him in town." She paused. "Yes. Just between girls, could you tell me if anything ever happened between you two?" She paused. "Oh, besides the pantry at the retirement home. I was there for that one."

Gabe's pulse pounded in his temples. He'd put his future in the hands of a woman he didn't know and whose advances he had rejected. What kind of moron was he?

"I see." Lauren kicked at the snow, head bowed. "You offered to show him your what? And what did he say?"

The cameraman had a boom mic out and was sneaking up on her from behind.

"You had to ask yourself if he had a pulse, he was so lifeless during the conversation?" Lauren asked loudly into the phone. "As much interest in you as a codfish has in a bag of beans." She paused, listening intently. "Is he gay, you ask?" She flicked her coffee-brown eyes up at Gabe.

He frowned and shook his head thoughtfully in answer. He was definitely into girls.

"No, he's not gay," Lauren said. "I mean, I don't think so. Out of curiosity, on a scale from one to ten, his apparent attraction to you was a...zero. Gotcha. Thank you so much, Shannon, you're a lifesaver. Merry Christmas."

She put the phone back in her pocket. "Well, when she offered to show you her collection of vintage Christmas cards at her place, you turned her down flat. She even said she would throw in some Bing Crosby to sweeten the deal, but you still refused. No player I know would ever pass up such an opportunity."

Gabe couldn't come up with a reply. What the hell was she talking about?

"He's not good enough for you, Lauren," Cooper warned.

"We already established that. In your eyes, no one will ever be good enough for me. But I need you to let me live my life on my own. Figuratively of course, since I'm still stuck at your place for a few more days."

"That's a start for your dare," Gabe said.

"All right. Now for the rest. I'm going to be honest." She took a deep breath. The boom mic lowered to her line of vision. "This has been the most amazing week I have ever experienced. You drive me crazy. In all sorts of ways. This game of dares has been the most fun, wildest thing I've ever done. I'm so afraid that when you leave, normal life won't have any glitz or sparkle to it. The Christmas lights will go out and everything will be drab. But I can't move to Boston, not even to be with you. This is my home."

"We can take things one step at a time. When I said we could keep going the way we were, I didn't mean for you to be a booty call. Well, I did at first, but afterward, I wanted more," Gabe said. "Just because it's long distance and complicated doesn't mean we can't give it a try."

"I have one other thing to say. We have to treat each other and this connection we have as something precious. It might not be love yet, but if we don't treat it like it could be love, then it will never grow into anything at all," Lauren said. "Can you do that?"

"Only if you promise the same and make things more official."

"'Official' as in you want me to be your girlfriend?" she asked.

Aunt Jo let out a high-pitched 'Oh!'

"Do you want that?" he asked.

"I don't know. Maybe. That's as honest as I can be."

He went down on his knees in the snow in front of her. "Lauren," he said, voice low and heavy with emotion, "will you be my girlfriend? I'll beg if I have to, or dare you again out of turn, whatever it takes. Will you?"

She gazed down at him, hesitating. "Honestly?"

He nodded.

"Yes!"

He jumped up and lifted her into his arms, then kissed her. He was finally able to hold her out in the open and before everyone, and to show them and her what she meant to him.

Sandra leaned over to the cameraman. "Tell me you got all that."

He nodded, wiping away a tear.

Cooper growled something threatening about how he would be watching Gabe's every move, and Lauren said he'd better relax or she would tell their mother about some vase that was broken long ago.

Abby, Mildred, Aunt Jo, and people he didn't know were laughing and crying again, jostling to get closer and wish them good luck on their new adventure together.

Someone offered to host a Christmas Eve luncheon, and for everyone to follow in their cars.

As the crowd thinned, Sandra pushed her way to the front.

"Miss Hall," she asked, "when you say he drives you crazy, is that in an overpowering, sexual way?"

Cooper arrived from behind to take her by the arms and escort her off the snowy lawn and to the press van.

Lauren took Gabe's hand. "I'm freezing. We'd better get someplace warm or I'll catch pneumonia and die. I'm not as naturally hot as you are, you know."

"I don't know about that, but if you want to go somewhere else, we'll have to find a hotel room that isn't too expensive."

"That sounds about right to me," she said. "Boyfriend and girlfriend, then? So this means no more dares?"

"Why no more dares? I have plenty in mind I could use on

my new girlfriend." Gabe nibbled her neck, making her squirm from tickling her with his beard. "Question before we go, though. Did Shannon really say I showed as much interest in her as a codfish does a bag of beans?"

"She didn't exactly say that, no," Lauren said. A grin spread across her face.

"You didn't call her, did you?"

"Of course not. You said I could ask her or I could trust you." She cocked her head to the side, studying him. "I chose to trust you. But I had to do something to get Cooper off my case. He takes his big-brother duties much too seriously."

"You can trust me. Not everything is a game to me, I promise. That said, the next dare is yours and we have all night."

***

That evening, "Deck the Halls" played over and over in Lauren's head, and she snuggled deeper under the covers. The bed was cold and too big for her alone.

On Christmas Eve all was quiet and soft, like the snow had the town wrapped in white padding, and everyone else was already asleep.

""'Tis the season to be jolly, fa la la la, la la la la,'" she sang softly to herself. This certainly wasn't how she had envisioned spending her night. She pulled her pillow in tight for a hug. A hint of Gabe's cologne was on the pillowcase, and she buried her nose in it.

The door to the hotel room's bathroom swung open, and wisps of steam streamed out. A wet-haired Gabe smiled at her, towel cinched around his narrow waist. She melted a little as a drop of water ran down the ripples of his abs.

He held up a white, plastic bottle. "Would you believe I forgot I had this?"

"Forgot you had toiletries?"

He twisted off the cap and poured the contents in his hand. As he crossed the floor, the scents of creamy vanilla and Christmas spices wafted over her. She closed her eyes to sniff deeper. Eggnog.

"Remember now?" Gabe knelt on the bed next to her.

She tugged his towel off. "I think you lost something."

"Funny. I think I found something. Right here under the covers."

"The question remains of what you are going to do with that body oil," she said.

He peeled the covers back and cool air hit her bare skin, making her nipples tighten. His eyes went straight to her breasts. "Don't worry about me. I've got plenty of ideas. There's a score we need to even up."

As much as she wanted the oil on his chest—he had been stunning at the knitting society party—he was right. It was her turn.

"Are you going to dare me to do something?" She bit her lower lip and hoped he would.

"Not this time. I'm just going to rub this on you until you beg me to give you something more."

She pulled him down for a kiss. His oil-filled hand pressed into her chest, right above her heart, and tingling warmth spread through her body. Her Christmas wishes had all come true.

Epilogue

The letter from the mayor was in her mailbox when Lauren got home to her tiny apartment. She certainly hadn't been expecting anything from him on Valentine's Day, but she ripped it open eagerly. It must be news or dates for when they were starting to build the shelter.

A minute later, she was jumping up and down, giggling with happiness and wondering who she could celebrate with, since it was the middle of the week and Gabe was in Richmond, working long hours for the governor.

She'd have to call Abby, of course. And Shannon.

To hell with it. She'd give Gabe a call at the office—she couldn't wait until later.

Lauren kicked off her shoes and went in search for her phone, which shouldn't be hard to find in a one-bedroom place but for some reason was always tucked away in a strange corner.

She finally found it in the dirty-clothes basket. Before she could dial, though, someone pounded on the door. A dog barked excitedly.

She winced, stomach constricting, but ran to answer.

Throwing open the door, she screamed when a furry mass of teeth and energy jumped up to put his paws on her stomach and howl in triumph.

"Flick," she said sternly. "Down!"

Aunt Jo watched, chuckling, as Flick dropped to the ground to stare up at Lauren in silence, eyes filled with adoration.

"You know the neighbors get mad when you make too much noise," Lauren said. He blinked in abject desolation. He knew. He knew all about the neighbors who came by to complain and point fingers. She shook her head at him and patted her leg so he understood he could stand. "Did you hide my phone in the clothes basket? What's wrong with hiding your own toys?"

After Christmas, she and Gabe had gone back to the shelter to visit the scared mutt who huddled in his pen under the mistletoe. It had taken her a couple of weeks to work up the courage and to learn about taking care of dogs, but she was finally able to take him home with her and give him the affection he needed to heal.

Within a few days of staying with her in her apartment, he had completely transformed into a bouncing, playful, and loving pet.

Lauren gave Flick a scratch behind the ears and hugged her aunt Jo in greeting.

"Come inside, Aunt Jo. Where's Ralphie?"

"Oh, he won't leave Schwartz's side since the surgery. In fact, I better get back. He's liable to sit on him like a mother hen to keep him warm if I'm not there."

Aunt Jo, true to her word, had adopted the old, black Cocker Spaniel and two more kittens.

Schwartz had turned out to be more sick than old and had

a liver tumor. The vet was optimistic, however, and Aunt Jo decided to give surgery a chance. Her house was more crowded with animals than ever, but she still dog-sat Flick when Lauren was at work so he wouldn't be alone in the small apartment all day.

"Well, give them both a dog biscuit from me and I'll be by tomorrow at six-thirty as usual." She waved Aunt Jo good-bye and picked up her phone. She waggled her eyebrows at Flick. "Big news, Flick, my boy."

He herded her through the living room to the sofa while she called Gabe.

A phone jingled outside her door, piping "Deck the Halls." No way.

Flick vibrated, shaking from tail to nose. Only one person besides Lauren made the dog that happy. It was Valentine's Day, but he couldn't already be here from Richmond.

She rushed the door at the same time as Gabe opened and stepped in with a single rose in his hand and love in his eyes.

"Happy Valentine's Day."

Throwing her arms around his neck, she attacked his face with kisses. Flick tried to squeeze his squirmy body between them.

"What are you doing here?" she asked. "You can't take time off work. You just started."

"Yeah, I have some good news and some bad news about that. Remember how I was going to pay for our next vacation like a good sugar daddy?"

"Yes?"

He coughed. "Well, today the governor's office manager announced they were going to fire me if I didn't try and sue the organizers of the Sycamore Cove Animal Shelter Fundraiser Committee for posting defamatory and image-damaging photographs of myself during my volunteer work, in spite of the fact I had requested no pictures be posted."

"And?" she asked, stomach sinking fast.

"And so I quit, because there was no way in hell I was going to sue my girlfriend and the kind people of Sycamore Cove. I'm sorry, but I'm going to be broke pretty soon if I can't find another job. The good news is I can spend more time with you."

She took his head and pulled it way down to her breast. Stroking his bearded cheek, she said, "Let momma make it all right."

"Mmmm. Wouldn't that be nice?"

"No, I'm serious." She took the letter from the mayor and held it up. "I can be your sugar momma. The mayor is offering me a job for a ton of money. Well, a ton of money compared to what waitresses make and you can stay here to take care of Flick while I'm at work. I'll pay for everything."

He lifted his head. He took the letter and skimmed it. "You'll be working for the mayor?"

"Yeah, isn't that—?" She blinked. "And you just lost your job with the governor. I'm a total cretin. I'm so sorry, I—"

"Sorry that you got a great opportunity to do what you want and stop waitressing? Lauren, I'm so happy for you. Really, don't feel bad. I made my choices and life bit me in the ass. I'll get up and find something better. This is amazing. You're amazing."

"Thank you. This could be your chance to find something in town or close by. In the meantime, I'll take care of you." She ran a finger down his neck to his shirt to undo the top button. She licked her lips. "I'll take very good care of you, promise. And if you can't find anything in IT, I happen to know a semiprofessional male dancer who could show you the ropes. If you were thinking of changing your line of work, that is."

"Lauren, I think I might love you," he said.

Her heart skipped several beats. "I just might love you too."

He lifted her up. "I dare you to say it."

She wrapped her legs around his waist and whispered, "Careful, I'll dare you back."

"I'm counting on it." He threw her on the bed and started the dares.

The End

Acknowledgements

No man or woman is an island, so there are a host of wonderful people I would like to thank for helping me on my journey:

My dad, most especially, for encouraging me to keep writing even though you knew you wouldn't be allowed to read this book.

My husband for making my dream possible and your unending love and support.

The fabulous writers and readers I've met on Wattpad over the last two years. My friends, you've made me laugh out loud with your shenanigans and cry with happiness from your acts of kindness. Never in a thousand years would I have made it this far alone. I love every one of you!

And to City Owl Press for believing in my story. Thank you.

About the Author

Leigh W. Stuart was born and raised in Kansas City, Missouri, daughter to an English teacher. This may or may not explain her early affinity to reading books. Although she decided to be a writer by the age of six years old, she later talked herself out of it and went on to study French and German in college. She met her husband in Switzerland, where she studied abroad one year, and they now live there with their two children. Love of reading inevitably transformed into a love of writing and she is thrilled to begin a new adventure as an author of romance novels.

www. leighwstuart.com

About the Publisher

City Owl Press is a cutting edge indie publishing company, bringing the world of romance and speculative fiction to discerning readers.

www.cityowlpress.com

CPSIA information can be obtained
at www.ICGtesting.com
Printed in the USA
LVOW12s1812211216
518299LV00001B/24/P